"What game are you pl

I breathe a little faster.

I don't reply for a long moment, and William's gaze intently searches my face.

"Kiss me," I suddenly breathe. Just blurting it out.

It comes from somewhere very hidden, somewhere I never care to visit. But it's out in the open now. William's blue eyes widen slightly in shock, and my own lips part as the realization of what I just asked of him hits me.

He narrows his eyes, his nostrils flaring as his gaze dips to my mouth.

I hear him curse softly as he shifts his hold on me and drives his fingers into the fall of my hair. He leans closer and pulls me forward with one quick, strong jerk.

And just like that, our lips crash. Just like that, William crushes my mouth beneath his. His breath is hot. His skin is hotter.

He's kissing me like he's dying for it.

I'm kissing him back like it's the only chance I'll ever get.

But suddenly it's not enough.

Dear Reader,

Thank you so much for picking up *BIG SHOT*! There's something so irresistible about a sexy bachelor with a baby, even more so when a sexy bachelor (with a baby) is brought to his knees by love. William Walker is a workaholic with a difficult personality, but when a baby comes into the picture, other facets of his personality start to shine through. Enough for our heroine, India, who truly believes that she hates him, to start to desire, admire and want him more than she *ever* thought possible. I just couldn't wait to share William and India's story and hope you enjoy reading it as much as I enjoyed writing it.

Katy

KATY EVANS

BIG SHOT

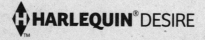

Recycling programs
for this product may
not exist in your area.

ISBN-13: 978-1-335-60379-1

BIG SHOT

Copyright © 2019 by Katy Evans

Printed in U.S.A.
www.Harlequin.com

New York Times, *USA TODAY* and *Wall Street Journal*
bestselling author **Katy Evans** writes swoony
contemporary romances with heroes to die for and
heroines you root for. She lives with her husband,
two kids and their beloved dogs. To find out more
about her and her books, visit her pages. She'd love
to hear from you.

www.KatyEvans.net

www.Facebook.com/AuthorKatyEvans

Twitter: @AuthorKatyEvans

www.BookBub.com/Authors/Katy-Evans

Books by Katy Evans

Harlequin Desire

BOSS
BIG SHOT

You can find Katy Evans on Facebook,
along with other Harlequin Desire authors,
at Facebook.com/harlequindesireauthors!

To my readers. You are all big shots.

One

India

There are three things in life that really bug me. The first is having a natural sleep cycle that wakes me up every day at 5:00 a.m. without fail, even on the weekends. The second is the fact that this rule doesn't apply to everyone: watching my roommate, Montana, glide into the kitchen for breakfast at 8:00 a.m. every morning, fresh-faced and ready for the day, while I've already been awake for three hours, never fails to make me groan. But my third and final pet peeve is by far the worst.

I hate my boss.

My demanding, stone-hearted, arrogant bastard boss.

You know those people in an elevator who click the close button repeatedly when they see someone coming just to avoid human contact? You know what?

That's my boss. But worse.

It's just past 5:00 a.m.

I've been awake for several minutes and I haven't yet attempted to get out of bed. All I can think about is the fact that I have to spend my day in the presence of the pompous pretty boy, William Walker. Ever since I became his assistant a year back, he's made my life hell. Now I wake up each morning at this ungodly hour and try to think of ways to get out of work and not get fired.

Call in sick?

Paint a bruise on my forehead and say I fell?

Say that my dog didn't eat just my homework, but ate *me*?

Tough. I don't *have* a dog. And it's not college anymore.

And William Walker is worse than any college professor I ever had to face.

Worse than *anyone* I ever had to face.

Voldemort, but very hot.

The minutes tick by. I sigh and get out of bed, dressing in my usual gray pantsuit for the day ahead. It's my standard work uniform at Walker Industries. It's not like I want to impress my boss with my clothes anyway. I want to impress him with my work ethic—or at least I did. Until I realized he was oblivious.

After dressing, washing my face and brushing my hair, I head to the kitchen and start up the coffee maker. The kitchen is the nicest part of the apartment because my roomie, Montana, loves baking. I glance wistfully at her bedroom door with a smile, wishing she was up so she'd bake something delicious.

Knowing she won't be out for hours yet, I grab my coffee and settle on a bar stool with my laptop. I've spent countless mornings in this kitchen with my laptop, sipping coffee and getting sucked into writing my novel. It's a blessing and a curse to be up this early. It might be a lonely hour, but it's the perfect time to write.

I am pulled into my story almost right away. My creative juices are flowing this morning, to say the least. My fingers have a mind of their own, flying over the keyboard at high speed. Before I know it, I have five hundred new words on my screen.

I have no idea if any of what I've written is good, and the perfectionist in me is desperately tempted to go back and correct my mistakes, but I learned long ago to ignore the nagging voices in my head. If I ever want to finish my novel, I know I have to let the words flow. I can go back later and make everything perfect.

It's part of what I love about the whole process.

It's easy to forget work and nightmare bosses while I'm writing. But the second I hear Montana's alarm clock, I know my time of peace and quiet is over. I've gotten a lot done this morning, but I ache to be able to continue. The last thing I want is a reminder that I have to see William Walker today.

"Morning, sunshine," Montana says to me as she breezes into the kitchen, heading straight to the fridge to gather ingredients for a pre-workout smoothie. Her black hair is slicked back in a neat ponytail and her face is fresh, with her golden skin untainted by makeup. She looks flawless, even though she's just tumbled out of bed.

"Morning, Beautiful Unicorn Morning Person," I say with a smile, closing my laptop. Montana laughs, glancing over her shoulder at me.

"Get any words in?" she asks hopefully.

"Tons. I'm happy it's flowing, just sad I need to stop. Are you going for a run?"

She checks her watch. "If I can squeeze it in. I have to be at the bakery at eight today."

Montana has been working at the nicest bakery in town for just under a year. It's not your average bread-and-pastry joint—it makes specialty patisserie items, wedding cakes and crazy showpieces like you'd see on a baking reality show. The food is expensive as hell, but the place is raking in money.

People in Chicago can't get enough. Neither can I, now that she brings me stuff from there all of the time.

Montana has a career that she loves, the body of a goddess and the best personality of anyone I've ever met. It's safe to say she's the full package, and it's still impossible to be jealous of her because she's also super nice. She's my sister from another mother, and she totally deserves the best.

"I'm sure your body would forgive you for missing one workout," I tease, sticking my tongue out.

Montana laughs. "Oh, nooooo, I couldn't. That attitude leads to laziness, right? If I don't go now, I'll go this evening. Do you want to come?"

I immediately raise my hands, palms out. "No, thanks. I'll get my exercise running to the coffee machine."

Montana laughs and piles a bunch of ingredients into the blender. "You know I hate the idea of you sticking around that job with the monster you work for. 'Man of Stone.' I mean that was the title of the magazine profile I just read in *Business Insider*. Does the guy even smile?"

I snort. "Never."

Montana laughs, then squirms a little. "India, you know I love you. I just think this job is really hard on you. I mean just two nights ago the guy was calling you at—what? What time was it when I heard your cell phone ring all the way in my room? 3:00 a.m.?"

"William's a workaholic. He doesn't know when to stop. He thinks nobody sleeps when he isn't sleeping," I say, wondering why I'm defending him when I hate the guy's guts. *Intensely.*

"I just thought maybe… Well, I don't want to see those circles under your eyes anymore, Indy."

I smile wanly, tucking my laptop away. "Trust me, I don't like it either. But this job is my lifeline. It's the reason I can still afford to feed myself while I write my novel. It's the reason I *haven't* become completely miserable, even if I hate my job." I frown at Montana.

"Look, we can't all love our job. I appreciate the thought, but I'm just fine. Anyway, I'll be out of there in no time because this book is going to be big," I say optimistically.

Montana returns my smile as she switches on the blender. "You know, if you want something different, I could try and get you a job at the bakery."

I groan. "Montana, we both know that's not going to happen. I can barely toast bread, let alone fancy cakes." I shake my head, picking up my shoes. "Just forget we had this conversation, okay? I'm fine. Everyone has to work a shitty job at some point in their life."

Montana nods absently, but we both end up laughing because we know she can't really relate.

Before the bakery, she worked as a personal trainer at the local gym. Before that she helped out in her mother's dance studio, teaching kids dance routines to "Twinkle, Twinkle, Little Star" and Disney Channel theme songs. She's never worked in a café, washing pots and pans, or as a house cleaner or cashier. She's always liked her jobs, and once admitted to me how she hadn't realized how lucky she was until she heard from others—like me—who didn't have it as easy.

Montana is in the process of carefully pouring her smoothie into a glass, biting her lip in concentration. "Okay. But if you're staying there, don't take any more shit from the guy. Give him hell if he deserves it and remember who is the ultimate boss of you, Indy. It's *you*."

I nod, forcing a smile so fake that I'm surprised my roomie doesn't notice.

"Well, that's some great advice, Mon," I say, eager to stop talking about work. "Thanks for that. I'll see you later, okay?"

Montana beams at me, sipping her smoothie through a pink straw and waving with her free hand. "All right, sweetie. Have a great day at the office. Love you!"

"Love you too!" I leave the room, acutely aware that each step I take to my front door takes me closer to the office. Closer to William Walker, the man they say has a heart of stone. Oh, yes. Every inch of that guy is rock-hard, heart included.

I almost shiver at the thought of the way he looks in his suits. Shiver from dread, that is.

Yes. *Yes*, it's definitely dread. I could *not* be so masochistic that I'd shiver for other reasons.

So I force myself to leave the apartment and head for the train station. The commute to work is short—too short. It gets me to hell far too fast.

Want to know something funny?

I usually spend it thinking of ways that I can wind my boss up and still keep my job. It's not easy, but I can be subtle. I have nothing better to do with my time between filing papers, answering the phone and making sure everything is perfect for a man who's impossible to please.

Sometimes, in the few free minutes I have each day, I daydream about putting a pinch of salt in his coffee or putting all of his files in the wrong place, though the perfectionist in me would never actually perform this prank. In fact I never carry out any of these fantasies. I do have some regard for my job and how lucky I am to have it. But on mornings such as this, a girl can dream.

My mother has often grilled me about my job. When I describe William's abuses, she always seems to think that I'm overreacting. She drones on about how she saw him in *Business Insider* and how handsome he looked. She tells me that his stern attitude is the sign of a good boss. I half wish I could drag her to work with me, like a bring-your-parent-to-work day. Then she'd see. Then she'd understand.

Though she'd probably still say he's husband material.

Ha.

It's pretty funny.

I pity the woman who ever gets saddled with him.

He may be a billionaire, but he's got a billion walls up around him, and a girl would pass out and die before scaling the first few.

I emerge from the Chicago "L" station to the usual windy morning in the city, and there it is. The building I spend all day in. The home of Walker Industries, one of the biggest online-game companies in the country. Mom says I should feel proud to work for such a prestigious company. I should be proud to have been picked from hundreds of other hopeful women to be William Walker's assistant. But as I stare at the gargantuan building, I think I'd rather be cleaning toilets than walking inside right now.

Why? What's happened to me?

I was so excited when I was first hired by Walker Industries' human resources department. I wanted to learn, and in my opinion I would be learning from the very best if I got to work with William Walker. True, he had a reputation for being an ass, but he was a genius in every way that counted. He'd single-handedly built his company from the ground up. But the moment I turned up for my first day of work and I saw him seated at his desk, my knees went a little weak. The blue-eyed stare he gave me almost made me trip. I guess it wasn't the best way to make a good impression.

Trying to save face, I said good morning, and my voice came out shaky and nervous because I was intimidated by him. He just stared at me, his eyebrows drawing closer together as I spoke. His jaw clenched. His eyes slimmed to slits. He's been a dick to me ever since, and I've hated my job more and more each day, for years.

Still, my feet carry me forward. I put on my brave face and nod to the workers gathered at the front desk. They shoot me smiles that are tainted with sympathy. They know what my job is and whom I work for. They return to their conversations, happy in the knowledge that they're not me.

I head for the elevator. There's no one else waiting—everyone here thinks they get bonus points for taking the stairs. But not me. Not when I'm thirty-two stories up, on the top floor. In the executive suite, with the owner and CEO. The big cheese. Top dog. Head honcho. Biggest asshole, aka Man of Stone.

Well, at least William isn't waiting for the elevator today. If he calmly pushes the close button one more time when he sees me approaching the elevator, running like crazy to make it on time, I just might kill him.

The top floor is relatively quiet. All of the most important people get stuck up here, and if they know what's good for them, they stay as quiet as possible. William hates to be disturbed. It makes it all the more tempting to create a disturbance, but I head to my office silently, not in the mood to cause trouble. I settle in my room, which is essentially a glass box. I've gotten used to my sleek computer, my ultramodern desk and my breathtaking view of Chicago. In any other job, I'd probably appreciate these perks. But now it's just a reminder that I'm stuck here for the next eight hours.

As I settle in, I notice that William isn't around.

He's the kind of person who turns up early to work for no good reason. It's probably because he has no social life—he's a lone wolf, according to my mother, but to me that translates as he's an asshole with no friends. Despite the lackeys who follow him around everywhere, I know he doesn't have any real friends. After all, I control his calendar for personal appointments, and in truth there aren't many.

But where is he today? Not being early is like being late for him. Until he arrives there's little I can do, so I meander to the coffee machine and make a cup for myself. As the machine is churning up coffee beans, the elevator dings and William appears.

I'll admit, something about his presence always knocks the breath from me. He stalks forward, with three people following in his wake. His hair is perfectly slicked, his stubble trimmed close to his sharp jaw. His eyes are a shocking blue. I can picture him now on the front cover of *Business Insider*, his piercing eyes radiating confidence from the page. But today his eyes are clouded by anger.

He spots me waiting at the coffee machine. The whole office is watching as he stalks toward me with a bunch of papers in his arms. His colleagues struggle to keep up, and I discard my coffee, suddenly fearful of his glare. Did I do something wrong?

"Good morning, Mr. Walker—"

"Ah, but it's not really a good morning, is it, India," he growls.

He shoves the papers into my arms and I almost

topple over in surprise. "I need you to sort out this paperwork mess and I don't want to hear another word from you until it's done." When he stalks away without so much as a smile, I notice I've been holding my breath.

And this is why, despite his beauty, despite his money, despite his drive, I can't stand the man.

Two

William

Ever recognized a mistake the second you made it? I do all of the time. Most recently, several seconds ago, when I was rude to my assistant. The second I shoved the pile of paperwork into her hands, I knew I was being harsh. When I walked away without acknowledging my mistake, I knew I was unforgiveable.

But who cares, right? This is me now. I stalk away with my head held high, and no one is shocked or disappointed. This is what the people working for me expect. I cut through the BS and it's served me well for years. It's become the norm. I've made my bed and now I lie in it.

It's just the way things are.

I head to my office and shut the door before any-one can follow me inside. I need to be alone, but it's hard when this entire building is made of glass. My father suggested the design when I was busy building Walker Industries from the ground up. I didn't care about aesthetics at the time, so I went along with it. My father claimed it would promote a healthy work environment. He said that my employees would see me as accessible if they could view me at work in my office. Instead it makes me feel like I'm in a giant fishbowl, being judged left, right and center.

I sit down at my desk with an inaudible sigh, hop-ing I don't seem as stressed as I am. When I glance to my left, India has retreated to her office to deal with the paperwork I've given her. She glances my way and gives me a fake smile before sitting down and angling her chair away from me.

India is the only one who is clear about how much she dislikes me. I don't know if she intends to show her disgust, but it's written all over her face when-ever we interact. It's kind of a relief, in some ways. No one else has the guts to do anything but accept my behavior with grim determination. India might not say anything, but I know exactly what she's thinking.

William Walker is a total bastard.

I sit at my desk for a long time without doing anything. I can't think straight. Not after the news I received this morning. My little brother, Kit, the screwup of the family, welcomed a child into the world a few months ago, which was hard enough to accept. As if it wasn't enough that he's got the perfect wife. Now the new feature he's released at Cupid's Arrow, my father's company and now the world's leading dating app, has earned Kit billionaire status. Which makes us equals in terms of our careers, despite how many more years I've put into Walker Industries than he has at Cupid's Arrow.

I can't figure out why I care. Maybe it's because I was always the successful one. Maybe it's because I've always taken some kind of pleasure in being compared to Kit. His mistakes only ever made me look better. Now all that's changed. Now we're on equal footing and I can't quite figure out how to handle that.

I'm selfish. How can I not find it in me to be proud of my brother, who has finally picked himself up out of the gutter and made something of himself? And then it clicks. He's managed to do everything I've done. He's done it quicker than I ever did. And he's come out the other end with everything I've ever wanted. Power. Status. Money.

Even his wife he met through working together at Cupid's Arrow. Now he has everything, including the perfect family.

Family.

It's the thing I've always craved above all else. My father and I have never been particularly close. He's British, as is Kit. Kit and I are brothers from different mothers. Mine is American and cultured. Kit's is British and a total mess. My father transplanted here when he met my mother, but he met Kit's mother on a fling when he was visiting family in Britain. Two divorces later, my father stayed in the US to raise Kit and me. My father and I…we spend a lot of time together, but it's a kind of business arrangement when I think about it. We talk about the company, we talk about money and shares and expenditures, and then we shake hands and go our separate ways.

He was always closer with Kit. Maybe because Kit is more like him in many ways—easygoing, not taking himself so seriously. Kit didn't spend his entire twenties trying to do everything right. He didn't try at anything at all—work, love or sobriety. None of it interested him. While I was busy climbing the career ladder, I almost missed the moment where that changed and he found his wife, Alex. Now he's got everything and I'm still single, wondering when I might get the same chance to change.

I have no trouble attracting women, but things never last. They think I'm arrogant, rude and difficult. And they might not be wrong. All of this time spent fighting tooth and nail to build Walker Industries into what it is today has turned my heart to stone. At least that's what people think.

I don't blame them, of course. I understand their reasoning. I know that when all I can talk about is the company I'm practically married to, my good looks and money can't save me.

My temper doesn't help.

I let the stress pile up and up until I crack and take it out on someone, like I did with India earlier. But I'm not a bad person. At least I hope I'm not. I've just lost the way a little and forgotten how to be good. I need a woman who will help me find the right path again.

I glance at India, who is typing away on her computer, her face devoid of emotion. She's a beautiful woman, with her tanned skin and a spray of freckles on her nose. Eyes the color of the coffee she drinks so often. Huge, wild curls that pass her dainty shoulders. It doesn't even matter that she dresses in drab clothes, because she always looks good.

I realize I'm staring and turn my attention to my computer. I really shouldn't be having any kind of thoughts about my assistant, but it's better than thinking about Kit.

I wonder what it would be like to have a woman like India in my life. She'd keep me on my toes, that's for sure. Even if she doesn't show it at work, I can tell she's got fire. She's smart as hell, organized and hardworking. A good worker. She's funny too. She always has the guys by the coffee machine in stitches with her cryptic comments.

But I wonder what she'd be like in a relationship. Pure fire in the bedroom, of course. Passionate in every respect, now that I think about it. I imagine she's the type who would hold grudges over little things and drown in jealousy when another woman shows interest. But I could be wrong. After all, I've never taken much time to get to know her.

Am I seriously fantasizing about the assistant I've done nothing but boss around? I shake my head. She would never be interested in me after the way I've treated her. Do I want to ask her out to dinner? Sure. Will I ever? Of course not. I know that even if it was appropriate, she'd definitely say no. What kind of girl wants to go out with the guy who makes her life miserable?

I hear her phone ring through the glass wall and she sighs loudly, picking up and putting on her best cheerful voice. She seems to relax a little as the person on the other end starts talking. She even laughs a little, leaning back in her chair and listening with interest. I roll my eyes. I already know who must be on the phone.

Kit.

I have to wait several minutes while India chats on the phone. Then she glances my way and says that she's going to put Kit through. She transfers the call and then turns away from me as quickly as she can.

The second I put the receiver to my ear, Kit starts talking.

"Hey, brother! Long time no speak. How's it going? I hope you're looking after that gem of an assistant of yours."

I roll my eyes. Kit barely ever gives me an opportunity to speak. It's usually how I end up doing something for him that I never agreed to. I sense now that if he's calling me, it must be in aid of getting something from me.

"What do you want, Kit?"

"What? Am I not allowed to call my wonderful brother for a chat now and then? Do you really think so little of me that you believe I'm only calling because I *need* something from you?"

"Yes."

Kit laughs. "All right, fair enough. I'll get down to business. You know it's Alex's and my honeymoon next week?"

I nod, even though he can't see me. He's not waiting for an answer anyway.

"Well, we've been waiting for this for months. After Alex and I got married…well, we thought it was best to save the honeymoon until after the Cupid's Arrow relaunch. Then Rosie came along, and we've wanted to have some time with her. So we've planned for this a lot. We had a babysitter set up. It took us months of interviews to find someone we were comfortable leaving her with. But she's had a family emergency and can't do it."

I sigh, leaning back in my chair. "What do you want from me?"

"Look, you're Rosie's uncle. We're…family, Will. And family sticks together. You know how distrustful Alex is about strangers around our Rosie. And we've both seen how much you've taken to her when you've come over. We were hoping you might step up and spend some time with her while we're away. It's two weeks, bro. We'd really appreciate it."

"I'd have to take time away from the company. I can't take a vacation whenever I want, Kit. I'm the chairman and CEO."

"Work from home!"

"And juggle running an entire business with looking after a child? I don't think so."

Kit sighs. "Come on. You're my only hope. Alex won't have a stranger babysitting Rosie—she'll cancel on me if you don't agree."

"What about Dad? Have you asked him?"

"Hell no. She'll wear him down in a couple of hours, and Dad was awful at changing diapers with us. Come on! You've got *youth* going for you, William! And I know by the silly grin you get on your face when you see her that you really want to do this. William, we're asking *you*. Are you seriously trying to wriggle out of this? I thought you'd jump at the chance to spend more time with Rosie."

Part of me loves the idea. I can't deny that Rosie is adorable. She gurgles with glee every time I'm around, and she's one of the sweetest kids I've ever come across. But looking after her would also be a painful reminder of what I don't have. Plus I meant what I said about the company. I've got my priorities straight, and Walker Industries will always remain at number one.

"Kit, I can't do it. You'll have to find someone else."

"What's that I heard? You'd love to take care of Rosie for the full two weeks?"

"Kit…"

"Oh, that's great, William. You're the best brother ever."

"I swear—"

"I'll drop her off at 7:00 a.m., next Monday. So glad you agreed to this. Much love. Bye, bro."

"Kit, you little—"

The line goes dead. I groan in frustration, putting the phone down and resting my head on the table.

How the hell am I going to get out of this one?

Three

India

Something is seriously off with William today. I haven't spoken to him all day, but I can just tell. I mean it's not like I have a lot of spare time on my hands between confirming his appointments and handling all of his calls, paperwork and expenses. But every time I glance William's way, he's pacing, muttering to himself or scrunching pieces of paper in his palm.

Something has wound him up, and for once it's not me.

I spend the day keeping an eye on him through my peripheral vision. After all, when your boss is in a bad mood, it's good to be alert. But when five o'clock rolls around, William is the first out the door. Which is also weird for him. But whatever. The workday has now ended. I'm not paid to care about what's going on in his head.

I feel a weight lift from my chest as I leave the office. I guess most people feel relief to be going home at the end of a workday, but for me the feeling is incomparable. In the back of my head there's an hourglass with sand running fast, marking the time to my next shift, but for a few minutes I can enjoy the fact that I'm out of that hellhole.

I guess part of the reason today hit me so hard was that William embarrassed me this morning. At least usually when he's brusque with me, it's in the privacy of his office. But today he patronized me in front of his entire team. And what did I do? I stood there and took it like an idiot.

Has it ever occurred to me to stand up for myself? Of course it has. I frequently dream about putting William in his place. I have visions of yelling at him in front of everyone. I fantasize about telling him where to shove his BS. I imagine the day when I slap his smug face for his rudeness and everyone cheers because, of course, he totally deserves it. The one and only thing stopping me is the inevitability that I will be fired.

And that, well, I'm not violent. I'm just *creative*. Blame the writer in me for these fantasies of revenge.

When I arrive home, the apartment is quiet. Montana won't be home for a while, and I'm glad of it so I can de-stress with some writing time. I sit at the counter in the kitchen and open my laptop, hoping to get some quiet time to write. But before I can open my manuscript file, I notice that I have an email from an unfamiliar address. The subject line mentions a job.

I open the email in curiosity.

I can't remember applying for a job recently—I gave up on finding something better a while back. But anything seems better than working for something like William. I read the contents carefully.

Dear India,

Deepest apologies for our late response. Several months ago, you applied for the staff writer opening with us. Unfortunately that position has already been filled. However our team has reviewed your résumé and we believe you would be a great fit for another role. Your writing is quite impressive, and we believe you would be an excellent contributor to the health-and-beauty pages on our website.

While the position is freelance and you'd be paid on a per-article basis, it could lead to great places. It would be a good way for you to get your foot in the door. You would also be working remotely, so you can work to a schedule that suits you. If you believe this could be something that would interest you, please let us know.

Sincerely,
Lauren Garvey
Freelance World

Oh, my god.

I reread the email, remembering when I applied a long time ago. I can't believe that I'm not hallucinating, that this isn't part of my novel. But this is real. This is an opportunity. I chew my thumb thoughtfully, my stomach skipping in excitement. What would I rather do? Take a job I might enjoy and get paid less or keep working for a jerk and have some spare pocket change?

Montana chooses the perfect moment to get home. She waltzes into the kitchen, holding a white box, no doubt containing leftover cupcakes from the bakery. She beams at me.

"Hey, girl. How was your day?"

I swivel on my stool, beaming for the first time in a long time. "The usual. But it might be about to get better."

Montana opens the box and shoves them in my direction across the counter. "Spill. What's happening?"

I take a chocolate-frosted cupcake and carefully peel off the wrapper. "I just got a job offer. From a media company. They want me to discuss writing for them. I could work from home and maybe give up my assistant job."

Montana's eyes widen. "India, that's amazing! Tell me you're saying yes?"

"I'm tempted. But the money is probably less than I'm getting at Walker Industries…"

"Screw the money!" Montana says in a very un-

Montana-like way. "Look, money isn't everything. You'd still have enough to keep up with rent, right?"

"Right…"

"And you'd still have time to write your novel, right?"

"Right…"

"And you'd even get to work from home. Or any-where. That would be good, right?"

"I mean, yeah…" I grudgingly admit, still feel-ing a kernel of doubt in my stomach at the thought of leaving William.

Because, honestly, what other woman will be crazy enough to put up with him like I do?

But why do I care?

"So, what are you waiting for? Email them back and take the job!"

I bite my lip, still reluctant. I think of his arro-gant blue eyes, and my stomach twists even more at the thought of leaving the bastard. Which makes me even madder at him for enslaving me emotionally in ways I don't even think he's conscious of.

"I mean…should I be rushing into this so fast? I don't even know what kind of work I'd be dealing with yet. And I don't have much experience, really. What if I screw it up?" I ask Montana, truly confused.

She takes my hand. "I'm telling you now—you are *not* going to mess this up. I don't care if you don't have experience. I don't *care* if you don't think you can do this right now. You will figure it out as you go along. There's nothing you can do to ruin this chance for yourself…except not taking it."

She's right of course. She always is. I nod vigorously, as though trying to convince my body to keep up with my brain. I'm doing it. I'm doing it.

Inhaling for courage, then exhaling, I type up my response. Montana squeals and claps as I hit Send, and then I watch as she sneaks to the fridge and removes a bottle of champagne. I grin.

"Champagne? Really?"

"Yep. We're celebrating. Let's get trashed."

I laugh as Montana fetches two glasses for us.

"Don't you think we should take it easy? It's Thursday night. We've got work tomorrow."

Montana shrugs. "Not for me. I've got tomorrow off. And who cares if you show up a little hungover now, right? You've got a new job lined up. Come on… What do you think?"

It's not my style at all. Come to think of it, it's not Montana's either. We're good girls. We stick to schedules and plans and don't allow for chaos in our lives. What are we doing, getting drunk when I have to be at work at eight tomorrow?

But I'm too nervous about my decision, and I could use something to ease the stress. I'm going for it. Montana hands me a glass of bubbly and I grin, raising it up.

"Cheers."

I wake up Friday morning and bet it's 5:00 a.m., like clockwork. Except today, trying to open my eyes is like trying to lift rocks from my lids. I feel nauseous. My stomach is still protesting the copious amounts of champagne I drank last night.

I sit up in bed with a groan. I know I must be late for work. There's no way on earth that I managed to wake up on time. I glance at my watch and my heart seizes.

It's 8:43 a.m.

Body, oh body, you failed me!

I'm going to be late to work on the day I hand in my notice. Shit!

Still feeling worse for wear, I shower as quickly as I can, throw on some clothes and call a cab. No time for the "L" today.

I watch the streets pass outside the window with dizzying speed. This is not how I planned to leave Walker Industries. I pray that I can at least keep my dignity when I walk inside to hand in my notice.

My watch says that I'm forty minutes late. Not as bad as I expected, but I already know that William will be furious. I dash for the elevator as the receptionist at the front desk watches me in wonder. I furiously press the button in an attempt to make it move faster. Someone is yelling, "Hey! Hold the elevator—"

And oh, my god, I press the close button. "Sorry!" I yell as the doors seal shut.

The sooner I get this over with, the better.

I head straight for the top floor, fanning myself, trying to stop the sweat pouring from me, but when the doors open on the top floor, my skin is soaked.

I already know where William is. I can see him in his office with three men in business suits. I curse. I was meant to sit in on the meeting this morning to take notes. William is going to be even angrier than I anticipated. Still, there's no turning back now.

I stride with as much confidence as I can muster toward William's office. I watch his head tilt upward as he notices me. His professional meeting face melts into pure, unadulterated fury. He rises from his seat just as I reach his door. I don't wait for him to invite me inside; I just enter the lion's den.

The other men turn to see who's interrupting their meeting. I can hear my own breathing, heavy and loud in the otherwise silent room. William's jaw is set, his blue eyes gleaming.

"You're late," he snarls. I take a deep breath.

"Yes, I am."

"You need to change that attitude before I fire you on the spot," William snaps, not caring that the other men are listening to every word. Our eyes clash, my whole stomach churning in rage for how he always treats me like this. And that's the moment I realize how much I need to do this. I can't stay in a place where a man gets off on humiliating me.

"There's no need to fire me, *sir*," I reply, flashing him a smile that's sweet as sugar. "I fucking quit."

Four

William

W hat the hell?

I stare at India, wondering who the hell she thinks she is. She shows up here late, looking like she's been dragged through a bush backward and then she has the audacity to stand there and threaten to quit? I watch her intake of breath as I take a step toward her. To her credit, she keeps her head held high, her eyes never leaving mine even though her breathing quickens.

Just like my damn heartbeat.

"What did you just say to me?" I ask, my blood

boiling with rage and something else. Something I've never wanted to feel for her but can't seem to control.

The closer I get, the more her scent reaches and teases my nostrils. Damn her. Still, she tilts her head back, refusing to break our stare-off.

"You heard me. I quit," she says defiantly. I can feel my neck and jaw heating up. How dare she humiliate me in front of my clients? I push past her to open the door to my office.

"Out. Now," I tell her. She folds her arms, smirking a little. She's finally letting loose with the rebellious side I knew she had. At the worst possible time.

"You're not my boss anymore," she says, pouting a little. She looks cute as hell. It's kind of turning me on, which is annoying. I seriously need to focus.

"We need to talk about this. Wait in your office for me."

I push the door open and motion for her to leave.

India looks like she might protest, but after a few moments she does as I ask. She casts a defiant glare around the room before heading to her office. Behind me, one of my clients, Theodore, lets out a throaty chuckle.

"Looks like you've got a dangerous woman on your hands," he says, smirking. "Not ideal in an assistant, but—"

"Excuse me for a moment, gentlemen," I interrupt, not in the mood to hear this guy's leering comments. "If you'd like to read over the contracts in the meantime—

I'll be right back." I take a deep breath, hoping to keep my cool as I head out to speak with India.

She's pacing when I enter her office. Her face has taken on a grayish color, but I can tell she's still angry. She casts a glance back at my office and I see that the men are watching us. Great. An audience is the last thing I needed for this conversation. Still, I need to remind India of her place.

"Sit down, India," I say quietly, but firmly. She sinks into her chair, watching me carefully.

"India, you've been a good employee," I begin.

She looks surprised at the compliment, but she tries to keep a straight face.

Suddenly more nervous than when I'm facing an army of corporate suits, I shove my hands into my pants pockets and give her my most commanding look.

"Which is why I am willing to give you another chance here. It was rash of me to make that comment about firing you, and it was rash of you to consider quitting. After the way you've just embarrassed me, I would say you're lucky I'm feeling so generous."

India's face quickly flits from surprise to anger. "Generous? Are you serious, William?"

I frown. "You've displayed some pretty questionable behavior today, India. Not many people would give you a second chance."

"And what about all the second chances I've given you?" she counters.

"What the hell are you talking about?"

India laughs, shaking her head. "Of course. You

KATY EVANS   39

have no idea. No idea at all of the consequences of your actions. You treat me awfully and you expect me to have respect for you? To be grateful when you give me a second chance? You've shouted at me for being five minutes late in the past, William. *Five.* You've called my home in the middle of the night just because you can't find some paper that I *left on your desk* the day before. You dislike it when I serve your coffee black and dislike it when I add cream. Nothing I do can possibly please you. And never, ever, have I ever felt motivated to do better, because no matter what I do, it's never good enough for you. I'm done. So done with you and your bossing me around!"

I'm starting to get seriously annoyed now. "I've always been fair to you, India. Don't turn this around and make it about me."

India stands up, shaking her head. "Why am I still here? Why am I bothering to argue with a man who clearly has no idea how cruel he really is? Well, I don't need to be here anymore."

"You can't leave. You're my assistant."

"*Was* your assistant. Keyword—*was*. I just quit. In front of your clients, so there were witnesses."

"Don't be ridiculous. I don't have anyone else who can do the work."

India smiles smugly. "Not my problem anymore, *Mr. Walker.* Now, if you'll excuse me, I'm going home."

"India," I growl softly, a tone that usually has her jerking back around to do my bidding.

Instead she's gathering her stuff from the desk.

I can feel my eyes getting wider and wider by the second.

And just like that, she walks out.

Just.

Like.

That.

I narrow my eyes, confused by the urge I have to chase her.

Obviously I won't. There's nothing more that I can do. I watch as she walks out of the office. And part of me is relieved to see her go. Relieved to know I won't see those big, bright eyes nor the whole tempting package that is India Crowley anymore.

Fisting my hands at my sides, I watch her sashaying away and I know that she's too good for this place. Too good for running around after me. Too good for being boxed in with a man who treats her so badly. And as she leaves, I finally understand everything I've been doing wrong—here and in my love life. Why has it taken something so dramatic for me to understand that I'm the problem?

I head back to my office in a daze. As I open the door, my clients laugh at my expression. I stand in the doorway, unable to figure out how to respond.

"I tried to tell you, Mr. Walker," Theodore says with a grin. "Never mess with a powerful woman."

Driving home takes longer than usual. I hit a bad stint of traffic and am delayed for over an hour. It gives me a lot of time alone with my thoughts. Most of them center on India.

How could I have been so stupid? So cruel and manipulative and completely oblivious to my own selfish behavior? Now I've lost the best assistant I've ever had. Not just that—I've lost a huge chunk of my ego. I guess I deserve that much, at least.

But the woman pushes my buttons in ways no one else ever has.

I wonder what she'll do now. I'm concerned that she doesn't have a job to fall back on. Will she be able to keep up with her rent? Will she get a similar job elsewhere, or will she do something more with herself? I hate myself for wanting to know, but after she walked out like that, I just can't forget her. Something tells me that woman will be on my mind for some time.

I pull up in the driveway in front of my house. Not for the first time, I glance at the mansion before me and realize how big it is for just one person. Two stories tall with double ceilings, sweeping columns, large custom-made windows, thick wood doors and brass light fixtures. This is the product of years of hard work. Years of isolation and late nights at the office. I lock up my car and head inside.

Inside is pristine. The imported marble floors shine like mirrors. The windows are so clean, you think there's nothing between you and the exterior. My cleaner—a woman in her late fifties whom I barely ever see—must have been here. She's cleared all of my take-out cartons and organized all of my notes that I left scattered on the large oak desk in my study.

I decide after the day I've had that I could use a drink. I head to the fridge and find a bottle of champagne. It's been there for over a year—my father bought it to celebrate my birthday but canceled our plans to go to some company party of his instead. I spent that night in the hot tub on the roof, pretending I was content with ordering takeout. I didn't have any friends to invite along. Kit and Alex were busy. Heading up to the rooftop to get in the hot tub now feels more than a little like déjà vu.

The sun is setting over the Chicago skyline. I fire up the hot tub and strip naked. There's no one to see me up here anyway. I slip into the bubbles and close my eyes, but even with the jets massaging my knotted back, I can't seem to relax. It's like the feeling of trying to catch your breath after a long run. I try to concentrate on the sensations of the water against my skin, but all I can see running through my mind is India's face. The anger in her eyes.

The shock when I finally said something nice to her.

I don't like the idea that someone could feel so strongly about me. Especially when I know none of the emotions she's harboring are pleasant.

I'm so lost in my thoughts, it takes me a moment to realize my cell phone is buzzing.

After a few moments of deliberation, I ease out,

grab a towel, get my phone from inside and pick up. "Walker," I answer, not checking to see who was calling.

I can hear Rosie crying in the background and Alex trying to soothe her.

"Hey, brother. I didn't plan to call and pester. Honestly. But, William? I need this. We need to leave. Like, right now," Kit says. He sounds tired, concerned, and like he hates having to call me.

"And why are you...?"

"What do you mean *why*? You're my brother. Alex's sister has had an accident. I need to take her to see her. Alex is distraught. Are you really going to bail out on me when I need you?"

I inhale, frowning as a sliver of panic seizes my chest.

What do I even know about children? Is my brother insane? Or simply desperate? I wouldn't put it past Kit to be lying through his teeth in order to get me to agree just so he can go on his honeymoon worry-free.

"Look, Kit, it's not that I don't want to help out—"

"Good. We'll be by in an hour."

He's about to hang up when I stop him, the panic seizing me by the balls now. "Wait! So this is you asking me to babysit or telling me? Seriously?"

"I'm telling you, I need your bloody help."

I grit my molars. Remembering what happened with India. Knowing that I'm an asshole. That it's time to make a change. I see that now. Starting with my home life. I think about my brother, silent on the other end of the line. Would it really be so bad to spend some quality time with my niece? After all, I can't be fussy about the company I keep.

I stare out over my garden below. I'm already planning the games I can play with Rosie, sitting on the lawn. My quiet evenings are about to get much more interesting.

"Fine," I growl, almost too softly to be heard.

"Fine?" Kit repeats, obviously shocked.

I rethink my words for a minute.

Maybe I'm making a mistake. Without an assistant, my job is about to get only harder. And looking after a child is a 24/7 kind of arrangement. But I need this. This could be my opportunity to prove to myself—and everyone else—that I'm more than some moody workaholic who cares only about himself. This is my chance to make things good again, to remind myself there's more to me than work. I sip my champagne as the sun finally sets, and I finally relent.

"I'm serious. Bring on the babysitting," I answer.

Five

India

I'm doing this. I'm actually doing it. As I head for the elevator, I refuse to look behind me. I half expect William to try to follow me, but he doesn't. Before I know it, I'm out of the building and on my way to freedom.

The thrill doesn't last long. The good-girl part of me is in shock. Why did I have to make such a scene? Why did I have to quit in the most over-the-top way possible? But I already know the answer to that question.

Because he deserved it.

Still, I used all of my chances in one go. There's

no way in hell William will give me a reference now. Everything is riding on this writing job working out now. Suddenly freedom isn't so appetizing. My breathing is labored as I head for the train to go home. I can't panic. I have to remind myself that this is what I want. This is the start of my brand-new life.

So why am I so scared?

Arriving home to an empty apartment at midday feels wrong.

I feel sick, but now it has more to do with my anxiety than with my drinking last night. I open all of the windows and make myself coffee, feeling more than a little flustered. Knowing I have a full day to myself should be exciting. I still have to finalize the arrangements for my new job, but after that I could catch up on my favorite shows or get some serious writing done.

The trouble is that right now I don't want to do either of those things. I want to run back to that office and beg William to give me back my job. I want to get on my knees and pray for everything to go back to normal because the idea of chaos is making me feel sick. But I won't do that, no matter how tempting it is. I have some pride left, even in the face of fear and uncertainty. I know it won't work anyway. The second that I turned my back on William, I became an enemy of Walker Industries.

William is a proud, hard man. He won't ever forgive me for the things I said to him—even if they were true.

Now I'm on my own.

The day seems to pass in a blur.

I sit for long periods of time, doing nothing, with the TV on as a mere murmur in the background. I can't focus on doing anything productive. I should be figuring out what my new job will entail or brushing up my résumé. I should be doing *something* to counteract the fact that I lost my job today.

But I don't. I just sit and wallow in my own mistakes, waiting for Montana to come home and snap me out of the funk I've gotten myself into.

Montana finally arrives at half past five o'clock with a bunch of shopping bags in her hands. She spots me lounging on the sofa and the realization crosses her face.

"You did it, didn't you? You quit Walker Industries?"

I nod, still a little out of sorts. Montana drops her bags to the floor and immediately comes over to put an arm around me.

"Damn, India. I didn't think you would actually go through with it."

That's not a comforting statement. It makes me feel like I made a mistake. A huge mistake. Montana seems to realize her error and backtracks a little.

"I just mean it's a gutsy move. But it was the right thing to do. You can breathe now. You don't have to spend all your time somewhere you're not valued and happy."

"What if it's not so bad? What if I have made a

horrible mistake, just because I can't take a little snappiness from my boss?" *And the way he makes me nervous as hell...and breathless...*

How do I explain to her that I saw his vulnerability and it's tugged at my heart somehow?

"India, I know you. You're tough as nails. I know you wouldn't overreact to something like this. If you say he's a nightmare, then I'm sure he is. Which means you're better off jobless than stuck under some controlling bastard's thumb."

"You're right... It's just hard to think that way right now."

"I know. Quitting your job is a scary thing. But you'll be okay. You did it knowing you have a safe backup. You've done the right thing. Coffee?"

I smile. Montana thinks a drink is the answer to everything. "Thanks, but I have some."

Montana nods, giving me a quick kiss on the cheek before heading to pour herself a cup. I lean my head on the arm of the chair, still a little shell-shocked by the events of the day.

Montana returns with her coffee, while I hold my mug close to my chest. Both of us are silent. I sigh. Each time I think back to what happened in the office, one thing sticks in my mind. I decide that perhaps Montana can help me make sense of it.

"You want to know something strange?" I ask her. She sits up straight, tucking her legs underneath her on the sofa.

"Always."

I chew my lip. "Before I left, William said I was a good employee. I think… I think that's the kindest thing he's ever said to me the whole time I worked there."

Montana sniffs, looking wholly unimpressed. "Well, it's hardly a shining compliment, is it? He could've at least been a little more enthusiastic."

"Well, I suppose that's true. But you don't know him, Mon. He's a workaholic. For him to give a compliment is rare, but for him to give me a compliment about my work performance…well, that counts as high praise from him."

"What are you saying?"

"I just think that perhaps I misjudged his actions. Maybe he's always been cruel to be kind when it comes to me. Maybe he was hoping to encourage me by keeping me on my toes, pushing me to reach my potential."

Montana tuts, lightly slapping my arm. "I don't know why you would ever defend his behavior like that, India. Besides, even if that is true, isn't that kind of manipulative?"

I struggle to find a way to get my argument back on track. "I'm just saying, maybe he's not as bad as he comes across. I mean I hate the phrase *misunderstood* but maybe that's what he is. Misunderstood. He's under a lot of pressure, running such a high-profile company."

"Yeah, yeah. I get what you're saying. You're saying that he should be excused because he does incredible work. He must be so great because he handles it all with grace. Except he doesn't, does he? Hotshot or not, he's not a nice guy. You're lucky to be completely rid of him."

I sigh. Maybe bringing this up to Montana was a bad idea. She's never met the guy, so how could she possibly see my point of view? Though she's right— defending the guy who has made my life miserable doesn't reflect well on me. It makes me sound like I *like* being constantly beaten down by a man who thinks he's superior to me just because he got dealt a better hand in life.

But haven't I done the same to him? Sure, maybe he started the whole cycle by being harsh to me. But was it always that way, or did I drive him crazy with my snarky comments and poor attitude? He kept me around only because I was a good worker. Maybe in his mind I'm just as bad as he is in mine.

The thought gives me a sinking feeling in the pit of my stomach.

Montana can see that I'm torturing myself. She nudges my arm, looking concerned. "Hey. You're overthinking everything. You need to let it go. This is where your new life begins. Make the most of it."

She's right. I can't just mope around, second-guessing myself forever. I sit up straighter, rolling my shoulders to get comfortable. Then I grab my laptop and open my emails. There's a message from Lauren Garvey. I smile. This is it.

"Right. New life. Here we go."

Six

William

It's Saturday. Alex and Kit are on their way now to drop off Rosie. I'm stalking around the house, desperately trying to make sure that everything is clean and safe. Rosie can't even crawl yet, but part of me is still terrified that she'll somehow escape her crib and manage to hurt herself. I've hidden every wire in the house so she doesn't electrocute herself, along with anything that's fragile that she could break and cut herself with. I've put locks on the knife drawers to make sure she can't get in. I realize how insane my preparations are. She's literally still a baby. But it feels important to get this right. A small life will be in my hands.

Not to be dramatic or anything.

I decide there's not much more I can do, so I head downstairs to sit in the living room. I can't keep still, as my legs are bouncing up and down while I try to be patient for Rosie's arrival. I don't want to give in to nerves. That's when I start making stupid mistakes, and I can't afford to do that when the baby arrives. I rub at my throbbing forehead, wishing I had taken a pill to soothe my headache.

A knock at the door makes me jump. I leap up, brushing invisible creases out of my pants. I take a deep breath as I head for the door. I haven't felt this nervous since prom night, when I attempted to have my first kiss with the cutest girl in my year. Hopefully looking after Rosie is going to be a more successful endeavor.

When I open the door, Alex is standing with Rosie in her arms. My sister-in-law is not one for smiling much, but she looks miserable today. It's been a while since I last saw her, and she's lost weight. Her eyes are ringed with dark circles, and her hair is limp and unwashed. I blink twice, wondering if the woman standing before me is the same one I've always known. Is this what I'm going to look like after two weeks with Rosie?

Alex laughs at my expression. "Don't be fooled by the cute little face. She's a terror," she says, but her tone is fond. She kisses Rosie's forehead and pushes past me to get inside, holding the baby in her arms.

I glance down the driveway and spot Kit struggling with a bunch of baby supplies. I'm about to help out when my father appears from around the side of the car. He waves to me and I head over to say hi, wondering what he's doing here.

"Dad… I wasn't expecting you to be here."

My father smiles. Like Kit, he smiles easily. Alex and I take a little more coaxing, I guess. "Hey, son. Did you think I was going to miss this for the world? Seeing you with a baby?" He laughs heartily. "Well, given your track record with the ladies, it might be a while before you've got a kid of your own. I wanted to see you try out Daddy Daycare."

He and Kit are laughing at me now, and I force a smile, pretending to find it funny too.

"I promise to do as good a job as you, Dad," I shoot back, and Kit chokes and laughs even harder, probably remembering that Dad couldn't be left alone with either of us when we were babies because he'd panic about poop, vomit and our getting into trouble.

"Well, if you're making fun of my parenting when you two were little, then let me admit that I'm relieved you're taking care of precious little Rosie and not me," Dad says.

"Seriously, bro, thanks so much for doing this," Kit says when he finally stops laughing. He looks almost as tired as Alex, though some of his usual energy still shines through. "We really appreciate it, especially so last-minute. I'm hoping once Alex's sister is all better, we'll still be able to catch our honeymoon. But I guess we'll see how she is first."

Kit and my father start carrying everything into the house, and I follow them. They dump a crib, a playpen and piles of toys and supplies in the center of the living room. Alex is reclining on the sofa with Rosie in her arms. She closes her eyes, holding the small bundle close to her chest. It's a relaxing sight, though I can't imagine how many sleepless nights have led to this moment. I'm suddenly glad to be helping out, even if only for the sake of Alex's getting a break. She looks like she needs it.

Meanwhile my dad is checking out the house. He hasn't been here in quite some time—I guess now that he's retired, he'll have time to visit more often, if only I'd carve time out of my schedule to invite him over.

I try to gauge whether he's impressed, but as usual he's unreadable. He shrugs, almost to himself, before starting to unpack Rosie's things.

"So, you think you can handle the little princess all alone?" Dad asks, looking at one of Rosie's toys like it's an alien artifact. I nod.

"I've got this."

"And are you all set up to work from home?"

"Yes, Father. I'm thoroughly prepared." I refrain from telling my father that I'm winging it right now, because "winging it" isn't usually my style.

Dad claps my shoulder with his large hand. "I know, son. I don't doubt you."

It sounds like you do, I want to say, but I keep my mouth shut. Now isn't the time to be confrontational. No matter how much my family winds me up and teases me, I have to remain calm. That's how I've always dealt with them, and it's worked so far.

My father can't seem to stand that I'm not a partier like he was in his younger days. He worries I'm too much of a workaholic and too uptight, and he taunts me relentlessly about it. *There's more to life than work, Will,* he'll say. And to Kit, he used to say, *When are you going to take things seriously like your brother, William?* So I guess you can't ever win with him.

Alex sits up slowly, her eyes heavy. She holds Rosie out to me.

"Here. You should get used to holding her."

I'm reluctant to take her from Alex, somehow. It's been a while since I held my niece, and the thought makes me nervous. Still, I have to get used to it, so I gently lift Rosie from Alex's hands. She's heavier than I expected, but I quickly grow used to the weight of her in my arms. She snuffles softly and I rock her slowly, hoping I'm doing everything right. I look to Alex for confirmation, and though her eyes look heavy from no sleep, she seems nervous to leave her alone with me and starts rattling off things that may go wrong. So fast that my mind's spinning with her instructions.

"Well, that's everything we brought," Kit says after returning from another trip to the car. He claps his hands together. "I guess we should jet off. We still need to pack to catch our flight."

Alex shuts up, and I nod absentmindedly, smiling down at Rosie. She's so peaceful while she's asleep. I kind of want her to stay this way the entire time. Babies are lovely when they don't come with any personal responsibility. Now, as Alex and Kit prepare to leave, it hits me properly that I'm playing the role of dad for the next two weeks.

What could go wrong?

"Have a good time," I tell them, pulling Kit and then Alex in for a hug. She lets out a soft laugh.

"I just can't wait to see my sister. Make sure she's okay. And then sleep," she says wearily, smiling. "I hope you took a long nap before we arrived. You won't get another chance."

I laugh, though Alex doesn't sound like she's joking. My father pats me on the back and shakes my hand.

"If you run into any issues, you can call me," he says. I nod, but I know I won't call him. Not even if the baby sets herself on fire or flings herself from a window. There's no way in hell I'm admitting to my dad at any point that I can't do this. No. This is a solo mission.

"Thanks, but no thanks. I'm going to be fine."

"And you think you can juggle all your work with

looking after Rosie?" my father asks, raising an eyebrow. I suck in air through my nose.

"I guess I'll have to prove to you that I can."

My father laughs, clapping me on the back again. "That's my boy. You always were competitive."

Only because you push me to compete with everyone. Including myself. Not for the first time, I realize that half of my conversations with my father happen only in my head. But I guess I like indulging him, humoring him by listening while also trying not to get hooked into what he says.

Maybe one day I'll have the courage to say all of this to his face. Alex kisses Rosie on the forehead as I cradle her.

"Take care of her," she says, almost pleading. She looks like she doesn't want to leave. Kit guides her to the door with a hand on the small of her back.

"We can rely on him, Alex. Let's not smother him."

"But—"

"Enough, Alex. It's time to go. I'll meet you at the car."

Alex takes a deep breath, glancing wistfully in Rosie's direction. Then, reluctantly, she heads out of the house, followed by my father. Kit grins at me, shoving his hands in his pockets.

"Don't take it personally. Alex hates leaving her, even for a few minutes. She needs to get away for a while. She's driving herself cuckoo."

I nod. "Just let her know that I can do this, okay?"

"I will. Thanks, bro."

I smile as Kit waves to me and heads out to the driveway. Though I know she won't remember, I take Rosie to the door to wave her parents off. As the car pulls away, I feel a pang of fear.

Now it's just me and Rosie.

I look down just in time to see her eyes flutter open. My heart freezes. Her tiny hands flail free from the blanket she's swaddled in. She blows a raspberry, getting spittle on her chin. She smiles for a brief moment and my heart warms. I hold her a little closer. How hard can this be?

I'm clearly about to find out. I watch Rosie's face darken. Her eyes droop. Her little lip wobbles and then suddenly she begins to scream. It's louder than I expected. Her face is bright red. There are tears and snot all over her face. I hold her at arm's length, wondering how something so small can make so much noise.

So…the nightmare begins.

It's been over an hour since Rosie started crying, and she hasn't stopped. I've tried everything to get her wailing under control. I've tried changing her diaper, but it was dry each time I checked. I've tried feeding her, but she's not interested. I've tried dangling her toys in front of her face, but she just ignores them. It's not helping my headache to say the least. I've completely abandoned the idea of work. How could I possibly concentrate with Rosie screaming so loudly that the windows are rattling?

I rock her back and forth, zoning out. I'm beginning to wonder if there's something actually wrong with her. Are babies meant to cry this much? I have no idea. I wish Alex had given me some kind of rulebook or manual. Instructions on how to deal with her wailing bundle of joy. But of course there are a million things that can go wrong with a baby. There are thousands of reasons why she could be crying. I just don't know what they are.

Then I spot something. Rosie's mouth is wide open as she cries. Her gums look a little raw. And it suddenly clicks what might be happening. I gently feel inside her mouth to see if my suspicion is right.

Yep. She's teething.

Great. Just what I need. For the two weeks that I'll be caring for her, she'll be going through what Kit once called the most stressful time for a baby. Why didn't Alex and Kit mention this? Maybe Alex *did* but I tuned her out because she sounded so stressed to part with the child. Still, Rosie may just be beginning to teethe, but it feels like an awful stroke of bad luck. Plus I'm almost certain that babies usually teeth at six months, not four. On the hunt for a solution, I put Rosie in her crib and try to concentrate on researching some remedies. After searching through the pile of supplies, I find teething rings and some teething gel. To my relief, when I rub the gel on Rosie's gums, she seems to calm down a little. When I pick her back up and help her with the teething ring, she stops crying for long enough to take the bait. I sigh with relief. The house feels oddly quiet now that she's calmed down, but I'm not complaining. Anything is better than her wailing.

I check the clock. It's been only half an hour, and I'm exhausted. Unfortunately the same cannot be said for Rosie. Now that she's not screaming, she's bored. I sit on the living room carpet with her, waving colorful toys in front of her face while she claps her hands in glee. It's definitely cuter than the screaming, but I haven't forgiven and forgotten quite yet. I just want her to go to sleep for a while so that I can get my mind together.

It's 11:00 p.m. by the time she starts to drop off to sleep. I watch her eyelids begin to droop and I jump on the opportunity before she can find something else to scream about. I take her up to my bedroom, where I have set up the crib, and lay her down for a nap. Within several minutes, she's asleep, and I sneak from the room without waking her up.

I head downstairs with the intention of sorting out all of Rosie's supplies, but one second after I sit down I end up sprawled on the couch with my eyes closed. How has a baby managed to exhaust me so quickly? Maybe it's because I'm aware of how far back she's set me with work. Maybe it's because her crying has somehow sapped all of my energy. Whatever it is, I'm beat. I can't imagine doing this every day for two weeks.

Maybe my father was right. Maybe I'm just not cut out for this. But then I remember something very important—Kit and Alex do this together. This is at least a two-person job. So maybe it wouldn't be so bad to have someone to help.

I need to call for backup. But who can I phone? Not my father. Not so soon either. I'd never hear the end of it. I guess the issue is that there's no one else who would come to my aid. My friends are mostly male and workaholics like me. I could hire someone, but how do I know I can trust them?

Trust is why I'm here in this position in the first place. Rosie's parents don't trust anyone enough to hire them, so if I do, won't I be betraying their wishes?

There's one other person I could call. I know she's reliable. She could help with my workload. She could be the other half of my parenting duo for a few weeks. She works harder than anyone I know, and is one of the few people whom I'd actually trust with anything. My company, my own personal needs, even her help in this. The trouble is getting her to agree.

Even though I know it's a long shot, I search my cell phone for India's number, exhaling when I find it. Readying for bed, I set my phone down on my nightstand, with her number on the screen. Ready to dial her tomorrow.

And refusing to dwell on the way my heart beats faster at the thought of her.

Seven

India

It's Sunday morning and I've finished work already. How did this happen? I got up at my usual time. I made breakfast and had a writing session in the kitchen. Then, after receiving my assignment via email, which was to write an article on the top-paying stay-at-home jobs online, I research and draft my story. Now I've been sitting around for an hour, trying to fill my time with minor editing and trying to figure out my next steps. I felt so productive this morning, and now there's nothing for me to do.

I sit back in my chair with a sigh. This isn't how I imagined freelancing would be. I almost email, asking for more work, but I don't want to appear as though I've rushed any of it. I scan through my writing again just to check that it's perfect, but the words blur before my eyes. I've read the article so many times that I practically know it by heart. I then try writing more on my novel, but when inspiration eludes me, I may as well accept that I'm done for the day.

I decide to make myself a healthy lunch. I steal some of Montana's salad ingredients from the fridge and construct a depressingly light chicken dish. It's so bland that it takes me almost half an hour to eat, but it's not nearly long enough. I still have the rest of the day, and if I don't find something to do I'll go crazy with boredom.

I'm reminded why I took an office job in the first place. I can't stay cooped up in the same place all day, every day. It doesn't allow my thoughts to breathe. I feel suffocated by the apartment. Desperate to escape the dullness of my first day, I grab my bag and head out the door without a second thought. I don't know where I'm going, but anywhere is better than here.

Now I understand why Montana loves running. As I race out into the street, I can feel the wind whipping at my hair. I cross the road to the park opposite my apartment building and jog over to a bench. I sit down, ever so slightly breathless, and allow fresh air to fill my lungs. But as I settle in my seat, I'm reminded that I can run where I want, but it won't keep me moving forward.

I know what I'm craving. I want to progress. I want to prove that I'm going places in my career and my life. Right now, quitting the office job and starting a new gig with less pay is feeling like a step backward, but with so much time to myself to think, it's impossible not to overthink it all. Now I'm stuck in a cycle of self-doubt, wondering when I'll finally figure out what to do with myself.

My phone vibrates in my pocket. I frown. I rarely get calls during the day. I come to the conclusion that it must be my mother and ignore it, but moments later the phone's ringing again. I sigh, sliding it from my pocket and checking the screen. My heart freezes.

It's William.

What the hell does he want?

My heart is suddenly beating a thousand beats a minute. I made it pretty clear that I don't work for him anymore. Is he going to try to convince me to come back? Is he going to try to get revenge? I don't know and I don't care. I don't want to speak to him. But the phone keeps ringing, and the more it rings, the more my heartbeat accelerates and the more I want to answer it. I want to hear what the idiot has to say.

I eventually give in and answer the phone. To my surprise, I can hear crying in the background. I frown. Surely William doesn't have children? I can't imagine anyone being crazy enough to do that with him.

"India? Finally. I've been calling for ages. Why didn't you pick up?"

"Hello to you too, Mr. Walker. Consider yourself lucky. I was thinking of ignoring the call."

William takes a deep breath, clearly trying to compose himself. I smile. I like that I can wind him up so much. I guess because he winds me up too.

"Look, I'm sorry to bother you," he says. "I wouldn't do it if it wasn't urgent. But I need you to come back and work for me."

I laugh in surprise. "Are you kidding me? I thought I made myself perfectly clear on Friday. I feel like I've made a lucky escape."

"I'm well aware of the conversation we had last week, but I have a situation on my hands."

"Yeah, I can sense that. What's with the wailing in the background?"

"I'm not in the office. I'm caring for my niece… for the next two weeks. Trust me, it was a last-minute deal and previously not on my plans. She's ah…well, she's a nightmare."

I smile to myself, thinking it's a little cute that he's babysitting his niece. Not as cute when the crying gets louder, though. It doesn't surprise me that William isn't good with children. He's not exactly the warm-and-inviting type. I imagine the poor child took one glance at him and hasn't stopped crying since. "Look, Mr. Walker, I don't really know what you expect me to do for you. I'm not a babysitter."

"I know that. I'm asking you to come back as

my assistant. I'm working from home, but between looking after the baby and trying to sleep and keeping on top of your assistant duties…well, there aren't enough hours in the day. I can't train a temp right now, and you know all the job details by heart."

"So what you're saying is that you want me to come back and do the job you practically fired me from?"

"You know that's what I'm asking." His voice is low, gruff. Almost pleading.

"Well, I'm sorry, Mr. Walker, but you'll have to find someone else. I have a new job now."

"Ah, yes. As a freelance writer, according to your LinkedIn. I bet they don't pay as well as I did."

I fold my arms and try not to let my annoyance come through in my tone of voice. "Yes, well. Some sacrifices are worth making."

"I'm sure that's true. But you could still continue with your work. I know that being my assistant can be demanding, but we'll be working from my home rather than the office, and I'll make sure you have some free time. Plus with the pay raise I'm offering… I think you'd do well to consider it."

I chew my lip. "How much of a pay raise are we talking?"

"I'll double your current pay. Plus I'll cover travel expenses to and from work, since I live in the Gold Coast. In fact, I'll send a car for you each morning."

Of course. The Gold Coast, where all of the mansions are.

I'm glad he's not here to see me roll my eyes. It's so typical that he'd use money and perks to try to entice me. But I have to admit, the raise is tempting. Two weeks of double pay from William plus the pay from my freelance-writing assignments…that would be a blessing in anyone's book. It would be good fallback money in case something goes wrong with my new job. There aren't any downsides. Except, of course, spending two weeks with my nightmare ex-boss and a screaming baby.

But can I really afford to turn this down? I know what Montana would say—that no amount of money can pay off unhappiness. That it's better to be short of cash than controlled by a manipulative man. But I can't help being tempted. William Walker has always tempted me, despite my resistance. Dammit. I take a deep breath.

"Fine. I'll do it."

William sighs in relief. "India, thank you. You don't know how much—"

"But I want three times my usual pay."

"What?"

I smile to myself. "Well, it's not like you can't afford it, Mr. Billionaire."

For a second I think I might have taken it too far. I hold my breath until he responds.

"Fine," he says quietly. He's clearly wound up, and suddenly I realize how desperate he must be. I guess juggling a billion-dollar business and caring for a child is a task and a half. I just hope he doesn't decide he can do it alone, after the bartering we've done. "I'll send a car for you tomorrow morning, India. Half past seven. My driver can take you home again at the usual time. You can dress business casual if you want, but I can't stress this enough—we'll maintain the same level of professionalism that we had at the office."

"Does that mean you'll be shouting at me constantly while I'm trying to get my work done?"

For the second time I wonder if I've taken it too far. There's silence on the other end of the line. But after several moments I hear a chuckle.

"All right, India. I'll let that one slip. I'll see you tomorrow."

He hangs up without saying goodbye. I slide my phone back into my pocket, releasing a breath I've been holding for some time. The call has left me exhilarated somehow. Maybe it's because I stuck up for myself, made demands, worked the scenario in my favor...

Or maybe it's because I was talking to William.

When Montana gets home, I'm thoroughly prepared to tell her about going back to work with William Walker. She senses something is off the second she sees me seated at the breakfast bar, with a smile on my face and a cup of tea ready for her. She takes it with a suspicious glare.

"I feel like you're buttering me up for something. What have you done?"

I chuckle nervously. "Well, I've done something a little random. Don't hate me."

Montana's glare intensifies. "Well, it depends what you've done, doesn't it, missy?"

I sigh. "Okay, I'll just say it. I'm going back to work for William Walker."

Montana slams her mug on the table. "What? Are you insane? You've only just escaped him and you're already crawling back to him?"

"Let me explain..."

"Well, this had better be a pretty darn good explanation, India."

"I've got him in the palm of my hand. He's in a predicament where he's looking after his niece and trying to run his business from home. He can't cope without an assistant, and it was too short notice to find someone new. I negotiated with him... He's giving me *three times* my usual pay. Let that sink in, Mon. Imagine what I can do with that kind of money."

Montana shakes her head. "Forget the money. I can't believe you'd go back to him. You're doing so well with your writing!"

"He said I can keep it up too. Which is even more income. Being his assistant is something I can do almost on automatic. I know that man and his rituals like the back of my hand. It'll help me fill the hours of the day, get me out of the house—because I'm seriously getting bored to death all cooped up here—and I'll be making a fortune. I know it's not completely ideal, considering I'll have to be around him, but otherwise it's an opportunity I can't pass up."

Montana shakes her head. "Well, obviously that's great. But what about your pride? Do you really want to be the kind of woman who will do anything for a mean boss like that?"

I shake my head. "Mon, it's not about pride… and it's not about the money either. It's just…it feels like progress. Maybe I can afford to save up, take a trip, finally get my novel finished and move forward with my life. And all it costs me is two weeks of my time. Two weeks in bad company, perhaps, but who knows? Maybe William and I will work out our differences and part on better terms. Can't you at least try to be happy for me?"

Montana looks worried. "I'm trying, but I'm not finding it easy. You know I just want what's best for you, right?"

I nudge her arm. "Of course I *know* that. And I appreciate it. But I can take care of myself. Better than you think. You don't need to baby me all the time. Hey, and maybe when this is over, we can take that girls' trip we've always talked about. Sun, sea, cocktails. Sound good?"

Montana's lips slowly form into a smile. "I mean, that does make this whole idea seem more appealing."

I grin. "Exactly."

"So, you start tomorrow?"

"That's right."

Montana chuckles quietly, but she's still shaking her head. "Well, I certainly hope you know what you're doing, honey."

"I do."

Montana sips her tea thoughtfully. "All right. But promise me one thing?"

"Sure."

Montana looks me in the eye with devilish glee. "If he gives you a hard time, promise you'll give him hell."

I smile. "Always."

Eight

William

A sleepless night will do bad things to a person.

Something I just discovered today.

Last night I fell asleep at 1:00 a.m., only to be woken up half an hour later by Rosie's screaming. First she was hungry. Then she soiled her diaper. Then her teeth were bothering her and I spent an hour supervising while she chewed on a teething ring.

I feel like I've aged twenty years in the past twenty hours. Now that morning is here, I know I have to get up and work. At least Rosie is currently sleeping. My driver is already on his way to pick up India.

And that's another thing. It's as though the Devil himself has planned out my next two weeks. I can't believe that I have to spend them with India. She has manipulated this to her advantage massively. Three times her usual pay? Ridiculous. Of course I can afford to pay it, but it's just the principle. She's a good assistant, but she's not *that* good. Still… I had no other option, so I guess whatever she wants, she gets from now on. The thought actually makes me smile a bit. Her ruthless bargaining would make her a good businesswoman.

But I don't like the idea of India's having so much power over me. She's a smart woman. I feel like she's going to squeeze all she can from me. She knows I can't refuse her demands, or she'll be straight out the door.

The doorbell rings and Rosie immediately starts crying again. I sigh. I should make a note to have everyone knock quietly instead of using the bell. I wearily drag myself up from the sofa to let India in.

She looks gorgeous today. Her curls are pulled up into a ponytail. She's wearing glasses with clear frames and her best suit. It takes me a moment to realize that she's mocking me. Making a point of turning up in business attire and fake glasses so she looks the part, even though I'm making her work from my home. She nudges her glasses to the end of her nose, pointedly looking me up and down.

"What happened to professionalism? No suit today?" India asks me.

I glance down. I'm still wearing only a T-shirt and boxers. Oh, well. I guess my tired mind didn't register something as menial as getting dressed. It occurs to me that I haven't brushed my teeth or hair either. India smirks, pushing past me. She's even carrying a new briefcase to complete her look.

"Let's get this over with, shall we?" she says. "And please put some pants on. That attire is entirely inappropriate for the workplace."

She's already trying to wind me up. Fantastic. Just what I need. I bite the inside of my cheek to prevent myself from saying anything. I don't want to give in to her games.

"Come up to my office. I've set up a phone for you, and a workstation."

"Lucky me," India says under her breath, flashing me a fake smile. I don't rise to the bait, ushering her to follow me.

We head through the living room to the stairs. I can sense India's holding back. At first I think she's doing it to annoy me, but then I catch her taking in her surroundings in wonder. She looks like she wants to say something about the artwork on the walls, the expensive rugs and the crystal chandelier in the foyer at the base of the staircase, but she doesn't. For once she manages to keep her mouth shut. But I can see the marvel in her eyes. It does something to me— something like making me want to impress her *more*.

Don't be ridiculous, Walker.

We head down the long landing to where my office is. I point her in the right direction.

"I need to go and tend to Rosie. Get yourself set up. I'll be there in a minute."

India nods absentmindedly, still distracted by her surroundings.

I leave her to it, rushing to fetch Rosie. I find her red-faced, with tears streaming down her cheeks, and her features screwed up, seemingly in agony. I scoop her up, hold her close to my chest and try to hush her. She refuses to be consoled.

I pace the room, rubbing her back while she wails in my ear. Her cries wake me up a little more, but they're also giving me a pretty bad headache.

I don't know how long I'm in the room, but it must be a while because all of a sudden India appears in the doorway, trying to tell me something.

"I can't hear you," I shout over Rosie's screams. India sighs, moving closer.

"I've got two clients on hold," she says close to my ear. Her breath tickles my skin and I have to stop myself from shivering. India winces as Rosie lets out an almost-feral scream. "Are you sure you have this under control?"

"She won't stop. She's inconsolable."

India sighs. "Here," she says, reaching out for Rosie. "Let me try."

I'm a little reluctant to hand Rosie over. She's my niece after all. I should be able to keep her happy, and not have to hand her off to my assistant. But at this point I'm willing to try anything to keep her quiet. But failing that, I think it would be pretty funny to see India try and fail to quiet her. So even though it feels like a failure, I hand Rosie to India.

India's face is soft and kind in a way I've never seen it before. Usually her expression is hardened, like she's constantly ready for an argument. I guess I must bring that attitude out in her.

Now she holds Rosie close and begins to hum. It's kind of tuneless, but somehow it seems to work in calming Rosie down. India carries on, perching on the edge of my bed and rocking the baby. It occurs to me that this is the first time a woman—other than my cleaner—has been in my room for a while. Not that the circumstances are particularly romantic—a screaming baby and an ex-employee don't make for a sexy environment. Still, I'm glad to have India here. Within minutes Rosie is calming down.

I stare in amazement at India.

"How…how the hell did you do that?"

India raises an eyebrow. "No cussing. Children present."

"That hardly counts as cussing."

"Whatever," she says smugly, smiling up at me. She continues swaying Rosie. "My mom always told me that when I was a baby, I was difficult to handle…"

"Still are," I mutter, but she doesn't seem fazed.

"She said the trick she learned was to always stay calm. That's what she did to end my tantrums." India shrugs.

"So that's why Rosie responds to you and not me?"

India shrugs again, a wicked smile spreading across her face, her dark eyes twinkling in ways that make me smile too. "Either that or she's just a good judge of character. She knows I'm cooler than you."

India catches a glimpse of my surprised expression and chuckles quietly, rolling her eyes. It occurs to me that I don't often see her laugh. "Chill out, Mr. Walker. It's just banter. Don't take it so seriously."

I want to argue back and tell her I'm not taking her too seriously, but it would kind of prove her point. I don't know why I care anyway. India is still just my assistant—and apparently a baby whisperer—but her doing this for me doesn't make us friends.

As Rosie falls asleep, India stands and gently places her back in the cradle. Then she straightens up, looking pleased with herself.

"Well, that's all taken care of." She turns to me, that soft expression still on her face, transfixing me. "You shouldn't keep your clients waiting."

I blink. I had forgotten completely about work. "Right. Yes, of course."

India cocks her head to the side. For once she doesn't look like she's about to bombard me with witty comments. She even looks a little concerned. "You don't look so good, boss. Do you need something? Food? Caffeine?"

I allow my shoulders to droop a little. "Caffeine. More than anything."

"All right. Let's get ourselves set up and then I'll take care of you."

India sets off down the corridor and I have no choice but to follow her lead. I almost have to jog to match her pace. She says nothing, keeping her gaze focused straight ahead of her.

"Is the office okay for you?" I ask awkwardly.

I don't like the silence between us. I'm used to having a wall of glass between us, and it always felt safer that way. No awkward small talk required. Now we're forced together whether we like it or not.

India snorts at my question. "Are you kidding? It's bigger than my entire apartment. Of course it's *okay.*"

I bite back a smile. I can't believe I thought she was going to make this easier for us. Doesn't she get that I hate this situation as much as she does? It doesn't matter how cute she is when she spends her whole time winding me up. "You know it wouldn't hurt to stop trying so hard to push my buttons."

India looks at me for several seconds. She seems shocked. "Oh, man, William. You blame me?" She shakes her head at me, all signs of humor vanishing from her face. "You got us caught in this vicious cycle," she says with a pointed jab of her finger in my direction. "I have a right to have my defenses up. If you want to change my attitude, try changing yours first. For longer than two minutes, that is."

She flounces off again, heading for the office.

Damn, that woman knows how to be sassy. I throw my hands up in exasperation.

"Don't I deserve a second chance?"

India snorts. "I'm here, aren't I?" is all she gives me. She definitely sounds irritated that she caved in to my request.

I watch her head into the office, acting like she owns it already. Damn this girl. I try to remain calm. It's just hard not to react when she's so good at getting under my skin.

But the next couple of weeks are all about proving what I'm worth. I'm proving I can be a good uncle. I'm proving my dedication to my job. But maybe I have an extra task on my hands—proving I'm not the horrible boss she sees me as.

I follow India inside the room. I find her behind the desk I set up for her. She has her work phone in hand and she's answering in that monotone she uses on business calls. She smiles at me as I enter, clearly smug that she can get away with murder now that I desperately need her help. But I force myself to smile back. She wants to break all of the rules in order to break me. She wants me to snap. Well, I'm never going to give her that satisfaction. I may have earned myself a reputation, but I can be patient when I need to be. And that is exactly how I'm going to handle this nightmare assistant I've let into my home.

"Yes, sir. Let me put you on hold. Mr. Walker's a little behind schedule today, but I'm sure he'll be with you…eventually," India says, casting an evil grin my way. I keep my cool as she presses the hold button. She swivels around on her chair like a child.

"Thanks so much for inviting me back to be your assistant," she says, her tone telling me how much she's enjoying this. "I'm having so much fun already."

I return her smile with one of my own. "I'm sure by the end of this we are going to be best friends," I say.

She doesn't need to know I'm lying.

Nine

India

Winding William up all day is actually kind of tiring. It's approaching midday and so far all I've managed to do is make his nostrils flare a bit after a slightly cruel quip at his expense. Otherwise I've been bombarded with work, juggling phone calls and managing William's schedule with my writing tasks for the other job. Now, feeling ready for a break, I glance at the clock and realize it's my lunch hour. Gleefully, I reach into my briefcase, looking for the leftover pasta that I usually bring to work for lunch.

The briefcase is empty.

I sigh in exasperation. Typical. I forgot to pack

lunch. I had one job to do this morning, and I couldn't even manage that. I was such a mess about coming back to work for William that all of my sense went out the window. I decide that I might as well just continue with work, but my stomach groans in protest, and I can't concentrate on anything else. Another of my pet peeves—being too hungry to focus.

William stretches and stands up with a groan. He looks tired as he picks up the coffee I made him earlier. It went cold an hour ago.

"I guess I should check on little Rosie," he says, more to himself than to me. He glances in my direction, almost as though he forgot I was here. "Did you bring any lunch or anything? You can take a break, you know."

I inhale slowly. I don't want to rely on him for anything. It's bad enough that I've come crawling back to this job. I don't want him to do anything else for me. But my stomach growls again and I can't help what comes out of my mouth next.

"I forgot my lunch."

I half expect him to point me to a store or to hand me a take-out menu to order from. But he just says, "I'm going to make something. I can whip something up for you too if you'd like?"

I raise an eyebrow. "You mean you'll cook for me?"

William blushes. "Well, I wouldn't go that far… I was going to make grilled cheese."

I almost smile. It doesn't surprise me that William isn't much of a cook. Not that I can talk, but

I've always imagined that William Walker has a chef to prepare his meals. I bet when he's left to his own devices, he lives off a diet of sandwiches and microwave dinners. But right about now grilled cheese sounds good.

"If it's not too much trouble…"

William rolls his eyes as he heads for the door. "Trouble? It's grilled cheese."

I almost reply with another witty comeback, but I stop myself at the last moment. After all, he's finally doing a nice thing for me. Perhaps he'll prove himself to me yet.

I follow him to his bedroom, standing in the doorway while he quietly checks on Rosie, who's asleep and looks adorable.

He lowers his voice and murmurs to her in dulcet tones. I like the way he is with her. Despite his inability to calm her down earlier, I can tell he'd be a good father. I mean he sucks at all other forms of social interaction, but being a father would definitely suit him.

He seems…human when he's with her.

More approachable.

It occurs to me suddenly that I'm standing in my boss's bedroom. It's a strange sensation. It's been a while since I was last in any man's bedroom, let alone William's. I glance around, looking for any signs of his personality in the decor, but the room is pretty bare. I make a note to check out the rest of the house. I want to find something here that gives me an insight into what William is like outside work. So far I have only a glimpse of the man he could be. I want to see the full picture before I judge how much to let my guard down. Because right now my guard wants to come tumbling down so hard and fast that I'm almost shaken by it.

After planting a tiny kiss on Rosie's forehead, William straightens up and turns to me. "Right. Operation lunch is a go."

I can feel the dazed look on my face and quickly plant a smile on my lips, almost laughing at his words. He's a bit of a nerd. I always knew that about him—he's too smart not to be.

I follow him downstairs, trying to act casual about being in such an incredible mansion. He leads me to the kitchen, a pristine room that is clearly rarely used. I sit down at the marble breakfast bar while William rummages through the fridge.

"I used to cook a lot," he says. "I just don't have the time for it anymore. When I get home from the office, it's just more work until I'm ready for bed, usually."

"I guess that makes sense. You get into work pretty early. But it's a little bit…well, sad. Don't you ever do anything with your spare time?"

William frowns without looking in my direction as he slices cheese for the sandwiches. "Free time?"

"Come on. Everyone has free time."

"I usually go to visit my father on Sundays. We

talk business, drink a little whiskey, have a meal. But I don't tend to find that very relaxing."

"Well, duh. Talking business doesn't count as downtime. What do you expect?"

William shrugs again. "I don't expect anything. A lot is expected of *me*."

At first I don't understand what he's getting at. Then it clicks. He never has any time to himself because he's too busy living up to other people's expectations. I study him carefully. He's the classic workaholic—driven, stressed and committed. He can't cope with standing still, and he would never pass up an opportunity to get ahead. That I can understand. I'm the same. But there's more to it. Is he doing it all to make himself feel better or to prove a point to someone? To prove that he can be the best of the best, no matter what life throws at him? I'm not sure.

"Well, from my point of view you're doing pretty damn well."

William chuckles quietly. His neck has turned red all of a sudden. "Thanks. Appreciated." He clears his throat. I can tell he's struggling for things to say, though I'm currently quite comfortable. It's nice getting to know him. Again, it occurs to me that there's a reason why a guy as hot as him can't keep a girlfriend.

"So, how is the new job going?" he asks. "Better than working for me?"

"Is that a joke? Did William Walker finally crack a joke?"

He glances back at me shyly. I find myself smiling at him before I can stop myself.

"I guess you could say that. But I also want to know the answer."

I sigh, propping my elbows on the counter so I can rest my chin in my hands. "It's okay. I guess I'm good at it. But I haven't gotten used to it yet. It's weird working alone all day. Kinda makes me crazy."

I wince to myself. Why am I telling him this? William, of all people? He doesn't need or want to know how my job is going. He's just making conversation. I shrug and smile awkwardly. "But it's fine."

William frowns. "So, you write blog articles?"

I fold my arms defensively. "I guess you could call it that. Does it matter?"

He shakes his head fiercely. "No, not at all. It's just…well, I assume you can do better for yourself. With your…skills."

"What do you mean?"

William throws his hands up in exasperation. "Look, I don't know. I just think that at some point something better is going to come your way. You're a smart woman. I know that much."

There he goes again, complimenting me. Is this him trying to make up for everything he did in the past? Is it just because I had a go at him and made him feel some remorse? As he slides the bread and cheese onto the stove-top grill and looks at me, I stare him down, wondering what his game is. Is he being nice for the right reasons, or is he trying to get something from me like he usually is?

William surprises me by taking a seat next to me at the counter. He chews at his thumb and I notice that the skin around his fingers is in tatters. Nervous tick? Clearly he's not as grounded as he makes out. Up close I can see how the stress has changed him, made his face crease with worry lines that I previously overlooked. Just by being close to him, watching him more carefully, I can tell there's more to him beneath the surface that I have yet to discover.

He also smells good. *Too* good.

"I hope you aren't offended by what I said," he continues, avoiding making eye contact with me. "I just wanted you to do the right thing for yourself."

"Well, everyone has to start somewhere, right? Not everyone has a rich father who can help them build a business."

William shoots me a playful glare. "Hey. I worked hard to get where I am now. I did it on my own without my father's money."

"Yeah, but without your family background, you wouldn't be where you are now." I hold my hands up in defense. "I'm not trying to belittle you. I'm just saying that's the way it is."

I can tell this conversation is winding William up. For once that's not the intent of my conversation. I just want him to see this from my perspective. But as his face grows redder, I know I've irritated him and that he really wants to argue back. Still, to his credit he remains calm.

I smile to myself. Now I know what his game is. He's trying to show that he can show self-restraint and be the perfect boss. That he is genuinely capable of being half-decent. Maybe I've brought out something in him that the people from the office never get to see. But my cynicism is deep-rooted, and I know that a complete change of character is far too much to ask from him.

William keeps his eyes on the table, but I can tell he wants to say something. I cock my head to the side, inviting him to speak his mind. He swallows, and I can see his Adam's apple bobbing as he does.

The next words out of his mouth are a complete shock. "I just want to say... I'm sorry if I ever mistreated you at the office." He pauses to clear his throat. "I know that I'm a difficult man. I know that you only ever did your best. I just never think before I speak. I speak plainly because my father raised me to always be honest. But often in the stress of the office, I feel myself being consumed by this...horrible anger and weariness, and I let it take over me without thinking about the consequences. I'm sorry that you had to suffer that every day. I'm trying to do better, like you said. But I'm glad that even if your writing work gets lonely, you have a job that fulfills you."

I don't think I've ever heard William say so much in one go. I'm used to short, staccato sentences from him in which he insults me in one way or another.

Now he's opened himself up like a book and put all of his insecurities on the table, and I don't know how to respond.

"You were pretty bad," I whisper before I can stop myself. William's eyes widen. He's clearly as shocked as I am. Then all of a sudden his face splits into a huge smile and he starts to laugh.

"At least you're honest," he says when he's stopped laughing. I crack a smile, finally feeling like we might be okay to joke around. I guess there's nothing to lose anyway. He needs me. Why shouldn't I speak my mind, mess with him a little, be as honest as I can?

"Damn right I am. I think you needed to hear it."

William's smile fades a little. "I think I did too. Thank you."

We smile awkwardly at each other for a few moments. He stares deeply into my eyes. My heart starts kicking against my ribs when briefly, very briefly, his eyes fall to my lips.

"There's something else too, India," he says, pulling his gaze back up to mine, a flush crawling up his thick, masculine neck. "Why I've been harder on you than—"

The timer on the stove goes off and we jump to attention. The moment is over. William scrambles from his seat to check on the sandwiches and I take a deep breath.

What was he going to say?

Do I want to know?

Being around William puts me on edge. He makes me feel like there's always something to be nervous about, even when he's not saying or doing anything. The tension in my shoulders won't leave until I go home today, but now that we're on slightly better terms, I allow my guard to slip a little.

Moments later there's a plate in front of me, and a tantalizing smell coming from it. The cheese is still bubbling from the heat, the bread is toasted to perfection and my stomach rumbles loudly. William catches my eye with a soft smile. Will I ever get used to this kind of civility from him?

"Hungry?"

"Starving."

"Eat up while it's hot."

I don't need to be told twice. I pick up my sandwich, letting it burn my fingers. I don't wait for it to cool down before I shove some in my mouth. I almost groan with pleasure, even when it burns my tongue.

"Doesn't everything just taste better when you're hungry?" I say through a mouthful of toast. William sits down, picking at his own grilled cheese.

"So, you're saying if you weren't hungry right now, my cooking would be unsatisfactory?"

I roll my eyes and smile. "I'm sure it would still be the best grilled cheese I've ever tasted."

William awkwardly takes a mocking bow in his seat. "Why, thank you." He pauses. "Maybe I should get back into cooking again. My ex loved it when I cooked for her."

I blink in surprise. Somehow it's kind of impossible to imagine William having a relationship. He may be hot, but he's also annoying as hell. Maybe that's the reason he's single now.

"Well, what did you cook for her?"

"Everything. She was a big foodie. She loved trying foreign cuisines. Thai food was a big favorite of hers." He pauses, staring at his hands. "I guess after a while together, I got lazy. Once the business really took off, I had less time and stopped doing nice things for her. Typical, right?"

It does sound typical of him. Classic workaholic. But he looks so sad right now that I don't want to make it any worse. After all, he's made an effort today. Maybe I should do the same. I take a deep breath, trying to think of a way to distract him.

"If it makes you feel better, my ex left me because I gave him food poisoning."

William raises his eyebrow a little. "Really? That doesn't seem like a reason to leave someone for good."

"Perhaps not...except it happened, like, three times. I'm a terrible cook. Every time I made him dinner, he'd spend the evening crouched over the toilet bowl."

William chuckles. "Sounds like you're a dream girlfriend, Miss Crowley."

For whatever reason, the comment makes me blush. William looks a little flushed too. We've gone from being enemies to joking about relationships. Is this conversation flirtatious? And if it is, am I encouraging my boss to flirt with me?

I cough pointedly and then shove the rest of my sandwich into my mouth. "That was so good," I mumble. I chew fast and swallow. Now that things have gotten awkward, I want nothing more than to get out of here. "I guess I should get back to work."

William frowns. "You still have half an hour of your lu—"

"It's okay. I feel like getting more work in. I'll see you back in the office."

I've never seen William look so confused. Frowning, he runs a hand through his gorgeously disheveled hair—something I need to thank Rosie for.

"I mean…okay. See you in a bit."

I can't leave the room fast enough. What's wrong with me? We're finally getting along and all of a sudden I can't handle a bit of banter? And then I realize the shift that's happened in me. I realize why I couldn't bear to stay.

I was actually starting to like being around him.

Ten

William

This day has been a roller coaster, to say the least. Spending time with India in the intimate space of my home has really messed with my head. One second she's cracking jokes, winding me up and making an effort to get along. The next she gives me the cold shoulder. I wonder if this hot-and-cold treatment is my fault. I suppose I spent most of the time being cold to her. Cold because I didn't want to feel the opposite way about her. Now I've got a taste of my own medicine.

She left an hour ago without properly saying goodbye. My chauffeur took her home. Now I suppose she's sitting in her apartment, telling her room-mate what a nightmare I am. I mean, at least I tried today. At least I made an effort to change. And for the most part, all she did was reject every effort of mine.

I don't care. Honestly.

I hear Rosie starting to fuss in her crib. I sigh wearily. I'm now at the level of exhaustion where my vision has blurred, and nothing feels quite real to me. But as Rosie's cries intensify, I revive a little and head off to tend to her. Unfortunately I have a feeling it's going to be another long night.

Rosie's kicking her legs in the air, her face flushed as she cries out for attention. I scoop her up and rock her gently. I try to take India's advice and stay calm, hoping it will soothe Rosie, but it doesn't appear to be enough. Either that or I'm doing something wrong. I bob her up and down, closing my eyes to try to block out her fussing.

This whole thing is a disaster. Why did I think it would be a good idea to bring India back in to work for me? Sure, I didn't have much of a choice. But now that we have spent our first day together, it's clear that she's too much of a handful. She only ever brings me trouble. Pushes my buttons. All the wrong ones. Hell, every single one.

I tell myself I don't want her near me. So why am I standing here now, wishing she'd come back?

I opened up to her. I told her things that I haven't spoken to anyone about. I guess when you keep everything in for so long, you need to have some kind of outlet, but speaking to her of all people? It seems like a bad idea the more I think about it. First off she's my employee. Second off she's a troublemaker. Third off I should know better than to think we're friends.

From now on, I'll keep it professional. I'll keep to myself. But that probably won't stop me from thinking of her.

I snap out of my thoughts and realize that Rosie has quietened down. She's dozing in my arms. I sigh with relief. If only it was always so simple to get her to sleep. I gently put her back in her crib and she still doesn't wake up. I wonder if I might finally be able to get some sleep, but as I'm heading to the bathroom to brush my teeth, my phone vibrates.

I sigh. It can be only one person. I get my phone out and answer the call. Video chat pops up on my screen.

"Hey, Kit."

"Brother!" Kit exclaims with a huge grin. He looks fresher already. He's in a bright room and I can hear soft music in the background. "Turns out Alex's sister had a broken wrist. She's out of the hospital and relaxing at home, so Alex and I are finally on that *honeymoon*." He beams, and a part of me resents him for looking so fresh while I'm beat, taking care of his daughter. "Just checking in from our *lovely* hotel. You look shattered, mate."

I attempt a smile, trying not to yawn. "Nah, I'm okay. I mean, I'm tired, but it's been a busy day."

"Yeah? You managed to fit your work schedule around our little princess?"

"Just about."

"Is she sleeping now?"

"Yeah, I've just put her back to bed."

"Dude, you're a dream babysitter. Though I admit, she does have a tendency to wake up at 3:00 a.m. and go full-on riot mode. There's a reason they call it the witching hour."

I nod absentmindedly. "Yeah, yeah. It's fine. I'll work around it."

Kit raises an eyebrow. "You okay, bro? Got something on your mind?"

I shrug. "It's just been a bit of a weird day. My assistant and I…well, we don't usually have to spend so much time together."

Kit grins. "Let me guess. You've spent a little more time in her company and you're starting to think there's chemistry there."

My heart freezes. Is it that obvious? Kit laughs at my expression.

"Dude, you forget that I've been through the same thing. When Alex and I first started spending time together, there were mixed signals everywhere. It's just natural. You're both attractive people. It doesn't have to mean anything."

But what if I want it to? I ask myself. What if what I've been feeling today, this crazy need to be around her more, is a chemical reaction to her presence? What if it's been so long that I've forgotten what it's like to be interested in someone? Is that what this is?

What if I'm sick and tired of ignoring this pull to her, this curiosity about her?

I rub at my eyes. I must just be overtired. This is ridiculous. "There's nothing going on, man. It's just a long day. She's a handful."

"Who? Rosie or India?"

I snort. "I'll leave that to you to figure out."

Kit laughs, throwing his head back. "Women, eh?"

"I can hear you guys, you idiots," Alex says in the background. He grins, glancing over his shoulder.

"Well, everyone knows you're a nightmare, honey. No point in denying that."

Alex throws a pillow at Kit and he laughs, dropping his phone to tackle her. Though the screen has gone black on the call, I can hear the pair of them laughing, presumably wrestling with one another. My smile fades. They sound happy. I can't help being envious of them right at this moment. I want what they have. And part of me wonders if this could be me and India.

The thought shocks me.

More shocking than the thought itself is the fact that it appeals to me.

Kit returns to his phone, breathless and smiling madly. He tries to catch his breath, but he's still laughing, shaking his head to himself.

"Hey, I'm gonna go. Kiss Rosie good-night from us. Let us know if you have any problems, yeah?"

"I mean…yeah, cool. Good night. I'll—"

The line goes dead before I can finish up. I'm surrounded by silence. Even Rosie isn't making a peep. I sigh, heading to the bathroom in a daze to brush my teeth. It's like I'm in a trance. And all I can think of is India Crowley.

This whole thing is ridiculous. I need to get it out of my system. I need to get *her* out of my system.

After turning on the shower and taking off my clothes, I step under the stream of water. I lift my head up and let the water wash over my face, my thoughts drifting. I think of the curl of her lip when she's about to say something sassy. I think of the way her collarbone protrudes from under her shirts. I imagine how she looks when she bends down to pick up a pen she's dropped. Little things I've been seeing all this time, but trying to never pay attention to.

I can picture her now, in the shower with me—her hair dampened by the water, a little makeup smudged on her face, her breasts covered in suds… I stop myself. The hot rush of water on my scalp snaps me back to reality. I know fantasizing about my assistant should feel wrong. But somehow it doesn't, which is even more unsettling.

What the hell is India doing to me?

Eleven

India

Arriving home from work, it feels as though everything has changed. It's later than I usually get home, but I don't mind so much. The car ride has given me time to think things over. To contemplate why William has gotten me in such a state. I've spent the past few hours feeling breathless, heart racing, palms sweating. I feel sick to my stomach, but in a way that isn't entirely horrible. It's a welcome feeling because I know it comes from a good place.

I think I'm developing a crush.

How long has it been since I felt this way? It's been a while. But this is crazy. Why am I going for a guy who has been making me miserable for over a year? Does it really take only one day for him to turn all of that around and make me fall for him? Or is it possible that we've just been acting out because we thought we had to keep our distance from each other?

Have we been misunderstanding each other this entire time?

Pushing back at each other to resist this pull between us?

It's on my mind for sure as I enter the apartment. Montana is on the sofa, with her hair wrapped up in a towel as she watches TV. She grins when she spots me.

"There you are, you little hard worker! How was it? Was it awful?"

I collapse onto the sofa in a daze. "Actually, no. It really wasn't."

Montana sits up straighter. She can always sense a shift in my mood, and right now she can see I've got gossip to spill. "What happened? Did he come on to you or something?"

I shake my head vigorously. "Of course not. He's my boss. It would be totally inappropriate."

"So is bullying your assistant to the point where she quits, right? So it's not like he's known for nice, appropriate behavior."

"It's nothing like that—I swear. He was perfectly civil."

"Then, what happened?"

I shake my head. "I can't really describe it. Everything was just...different."

"In a good way?"

I sigh dreamily. "Yes. In a very good way."

Montana frowns at me. "Okay, you're starting to freak me out with this vagueness. Spill the beans *right now*."

I twirl a strand of hair around my finger, refusing to look Montana in the eye. She's scarily intense when she's trying to get information out of me. "I just have a really good feeling about the next couple weeks, you know? I think maybe I got him entirely wrong."

"What makes you say that? Are you implying that you've been overreacting to him this whole time?"

"No, not really. I just think there's another side to him. A side that's not really visible in the office. He's proved today just how sweet and caring he can be."

"What, so one day of him acting innocent and you're convinced he's the perfect gentleman? India, did you hit your head on the way home or something? You're acting like a lovesick teenager."

I close my eyes with a smile. "It was just a good day, okay? I feel good about the whole thing."

Montana folds her arms, looking like a stern mother. "Listen to me, India. It's great that you and William have sorted out your differences or whatever. I'm happy for you—really. But please be careful. Men like him...they can manipulate you to feel a certain way. I just don't want you to fall into a trap."

"A trap? Really?"

"I'm serious. You don't know what his intentions are. He's got you alone in his house for two weeks. He might be trying to get you to sleep with him."

"He's babysitting his niece! He has to work from home. He can't exactly bring a baby into Walker Industries with him, can he?"

"I'm just saying, he might be using this as an opportunity to take advantage."

"If you knew him, you would realize that's ridiculous. He's, like, the least flirtatious man I've ever met. Just because I think there's some chemistry there, it doesn't mean that anything is going to happen. Besides, he's my boss. I'd never allow that to happen."

"It's just all a little unusual, Indy. You must be able to see that. I'm just worried about you being screwed over or something. You know I'd never want anything bad to happen to you."

I smile gently. "I know, Mon. I appreciate you looking out for me—I really do. But I think it's okay. It's just a silly little crush I've got on him, that's all. It's not going to lead anywhere, even if I wanted it to."

Montana nods, but she still looks a little concerned. "I mean, okay. I believe you. But I just want you to keep your wits about you."

I nod, standing up. This conversation has dampened my mood considerably. All of a sudden I just want to be alone. "Yeah, of course. I think I'll grab a shower and head to bed. I've had a long day."

Montana stares at me. "Indy, is everything okay?"

"Of course."

"Do you want—"

"Everything's fine," I assure her, faking a smile. Then I leave the room before she can question me more.

I get in the shower with my head in a whirl. Of course, as usual Montana is completely right. Why should I place any weight on these feelings after everything William has done? Why should I trust a man who has given me no reason to believe he's anything but a jerk up until today? How do I know his game anyway? Maybe this happens with him all of the time. Maybe he switches on the charm just to get women to like him and then returns to his usual self and starts pushing them around again after he gets his way. I don't want to believe it, but it's a possible scenario.

I shower for a long time, hoping the hot water will knock some sense into me. It doesn't. I head to bed, feeling tense and frustrated. I feel aroused, though I can't figure out why. Maybe it's because everything between William and me always seems to balance on a knife-edge. I never know what I might get when I'm around him. It keeps me on my toes. And now that the balance is shifting, it's getting me hot and bothered.

I wonder if he feels it too. I wonder if at lunch

today he sensed my attraction to him. I wonder if he knows he's winning at his little game.

Was I lying to Montana? Would I let anything develop if the opportunity arose? I want to believe I'd do the right thing. But as I snuggle my pillow and imagine I'm snuggling against his wide, strong chest, I'm not sure I was telling the truth.

My body feels tense. I can't stop remembering how close he was. Remembering the way he smells so clearly that it makes my mouth water and my body ache. I turn my pillow over and close my eyes. My whole body feels charged and buzzed. I imagine him kissing me.

I impulsively nuzzle my pillow as if it was his face and I nearly jolt. The physical contact of anything against my lips shocks me. It's been a while since I felt this sexual. I picture his fingers exploring my body, and I wish it was happening for real. I shouldn't be wanting this, feeling this hot. I shouldn't be fantasizing about my boss. But I can't help it. I want to. I want…him.

I groan and punch my pillow, trying to get him out of my mind. But a flash of him smiling at me only makes me ache harder.

A knock on the door shocks me to my senses. I jerk upright, blushing as I try to push my dirty thoughts about William Walker to the back of my mind.

"Yeah?"

Montana enters my room, holding two mugs.

"Hey. I thought you might like some hot chocolate before you go to bed."

"Oh. Thanks, Mon. That's really nice," I say. I wonder if she can tell what I've just been thinking. I wonder if I look as flustered as I feel. But she doesn't seem fazed. She simply puts the mug on my bedside table and sits on the edge of my bed, sipping her hot chocolate.

"Hey, I'm sorry if I bothered you before. I always feel kinda protective of you. You're my best friend, and I know despite the tough act you put on, you're all bark, no bite. I just don't want him to hurt you anymore."

I hike up my shoulders, trying to act normal while thoughts of William continue lingering in my brain. "I know, but he won't. Honestly."

Montana smiles sweetly. I wish she'd just leave, but she looks like she's got more to say. She takes a deep breath. "I was being a little overprotective before. But I trust you, India. I know you'll do the right thing and that you'll watch out for yourself. You always do."

I nod. "Yeah, I do. Thank you for watching out for me too." But I feel guilty. I know I'm looking my best friend in the eye and lying to her. Still, she hasn't picked up on my nerves. She stands up, taking another sip of her hot chocolate.

"Good, then. Good night, Indy."

I breathe again only after she's left the room. This is ridiculous. My emotions are all over the place

today. I switch off the light, abandoning my hot chocolate, and force myself to try to sleep, ignoring the
ache between my legs for something I shouldn't have.

I'm up earlier than usual this morning. It's only
half past four, and I can't get back to sleep. I decide
to skip my writing session for the morning, and instead I actually spend some time getting ready. I
put on my nicest suit, one that I've never worn for
work before. I take time taming my hair, putting on
makeup and choosing my favorite perfume. I've got
butterflies in my stomach, as though I am preparing for a date. It's a ridiculous notion. I'm heading
to work, for goodness' sake. But it doesn't stop me
from putting all of my efforts into how I look.

I'm ready by the time Montana is up. She offers
me breakfast, but I'm too wound up to eat anything.
When the chauffeur arrives, I've been sitting around
for a while, just waiting for him to get here. I think
secretly I was hoping he might be early, so that I'd
have more time with William. How ridiculous can
I get? He's my boss. Not my friend. Not my lover.
My *boss*.

I need a cold shower or something.

When I arrive, William is tending to Rosie, who
is crying. With his other hand, he's texting from his
work phone. I smile at him as I enter, the butterflies
in my stomach somehow increasing in intensity, but
all I get back is a curt nod. I frown to myself. Have

we really headed straight back to square one? Did I imagine yesterday?

I shouldn't have gotten my hopes up. I head upstairs to William's office and get settled in, but I can't stop thinking about everything I read wrong. All of the signals that I was doing something right, that we were finally getting somewhere…it was all fake. William and I were never moving forward. At best we were standing still, and that's the way it'll always be with the two of us.

William spends the day drifting in and out of the office. I try not to look in his direction, but as the day goes on, it gets harder and harder. He looks even more disheveled than yesterday, with his shirt buttoned up only halfway. I can see the ripples of his chest, and the outline of his collarbone. This morning, when I got here, his curls were still damp from the shower. The whole messy aesthetic has me holding my breath, holding my tongue, holding myself back from him. As lunch approaches, I excuse myself to get a glass of water before returning to my desk. Presumably, William has gone for lunch. Not that I care. I really don't.

It's nearly halfway through my break when I feel a gentle hand on my shoulder. The connection sends a shock of electricity through me, but I try to keep my cool. But the second I look up and see William's face, I have to gasp a little for air. For a wild second I think he's going to kiss me. But then, with a cheeky smile on his face, he hands me a plate. On it is a grilled cheese sandwich. I can't help but smile.

Not quite a kiss, but almost as good.

Twelve

William

The past few days have been a blur, but in a good way. They've been long and tiring, but among the diaper changes and boring conference calls, there's India. India, who lights up the room when she walks in. India, who sets my heart racing each time she smiles. India, who makes me laugh until my sides hurt. That's the woman I get to spend my days with.

How did I not see it earlier? How perfect she is. I spent so much time with my head up my own ass that I never realized what a gem she is. I never appreciated her—I never let myself—not as an employee and not as a person. Now it's all I see. She's all I think about.

Now it's Friday, and it's nearly time for her to head home. I can't believe I'm going to spend an entire weekend without her after spending so much time in her company the past several days.

She's packing up slowly, as though she doesn't want to leave either. Or perhaps I'm just imagining it, seeing what I want to see.

She's probably happy to be getting out of here. After all, she's got her whole weekend ahead of her. I wonder what she plans to do.

Maybe she and her friend Montana will hit the town after a bottle or two of rosé.

Maybe she prefers a night in on the couch, watching movies and eating popcorn that's hot from the microwave.

It's things like this that I want to ask her, so that I can figure her out. But I keep my mouth shut because I'm concerned about taking a step forward that I can't take back. What do I even know about formal relationships?

No woman I've ever tried to have a relationship with ever sticks around. I'm too much of a workaholic, and they want someone who prioritizes them first. That's not me.

Though I feel capable of shifting priorities since I've been able to put Rosie at the top spot for now, relationships and feelings are not my forte, and I'm reluctant to go there with my assistant. Even only in my thoughts.

She's finished packing up her laptop. She flashes me a smile.

"Well, I guess I'll see you on Monday," she says. I nod, trying to hide my disappointment. I don't want her to see the effect she's had on me this week.

"Yeah, perfect. Same time?"

"Sure." India starts toward the door, but she hesitates. She's holding her briefcase in front of her, looking nervous. She clears her throat. "Well, if you need a hand with Rosie at all…you know where I am. After all, I am pretty good with her now. And you'll want to sleep at some point…"

I smile. Is she really making excuses to come over? Maybe she's just being polite, but I sense that she isn't. That's not really her style.

She wants to stay.

I'm about to respond when my phone rings. I smile apologetically at India.

"Sorry. I've just got to take this."

I glance at the screen. It's my chauffeur, Henry. I pick up the call.

"Henry. Everything all right?" I ask. In the background, I can hear the loud sputtering of an engine. Henry sighs.

"Hey, boss. I've got a bit of a dilemma. The car broke down."

"Wait, what?"

"Yep. I don't know what the hell happened. I think

the engine overheated on the highway. I've called someone to come and take a look at it, but I won't be able to take India back to town yet."

I glance at India, who's standing before me, trying to read my expression. I feel like smiling, but I'm too skilled in the art of holding emotion back to let it slip. Still. This is good. It's almost as though it's fate. "Don't worry, Henry. I'll make alternative arrangements. Thanks for letting me know."

I hang up. India is watching me with a questioning look in her eyes.

"Is everything okay?"

"Henry won't be able to take you home today. At least not for a few hours."

India looks surprised. "Oh, right, I see. Should I take an Uber instead? I can be out of your way in, like, ten minutes."

She looks shy, hesitant. Vulnerable.

And I really want to grab her and kiss her. I want to tell her to stay here, with *me*. But I don't. Instead I clear my throat and glance at the floor. "Well, you could… I could drive you but I don't want to wake Rosie for the ride."

"Oh, no, of course not—"

"Or you can stay for dinner while we figure it out." India looks a little shocked at the idea and I feel myself blush.

I don't think I've ever seen her so caught off guard. I want to reach out and smooth my fingers down those flushed cheeks. But after a few moments she manages to compose herself, taking a deep breath.

"Yeah, okay. As long as you don't think I would be getting in the way…"

I smile at her, taking a step closer. Is it just my imagination, or is she holding her breath? I allow my hand to rest on her shoulder for a second. "You wouldn't be in the way at all," I insist. India visibly relaxes, putting down her briefcase.

"Okay. Well, might as well make myself useful."

I raise an eyebrow. "Useful?"

She fetches her phone from her pocket. "By looking up take-out menus, of course."

I grin. She really is a perfect woman. "Sounds like an idea. I'm just going to check on Rosie. Feel free to explore the house… Maybe you could pick out a film to watch while we eat."

India smiles. Her arm brushes against mine as she heads for the door. "Sounds cozy," she says with a devilish look in her eyes.

I distract myself from India for a while by tending to the baby. She's been surprisingly good the past few days, to the point where it's actually a little suspicious. She kicks her legs and waves her arms around when she sees me, gurgling loudly. I like to take that as an affectionate greeting. I scoop her up with a smile and nuzzle her closely. She smells good as I bounce her up and down.

"You're getting really good with her."

I turn and see India at the door. She's leaning on the door frame, smiling fondly. I smile.

"Yeah, well. I guess my uncle instincts have finally kicked in."

"Looks like it," she says. "I think you're doing a lot of self-improvement this week."

I roll my eyes. Now that we're getting along better, she takes every opportunity to make fun of how we were before. I keep reminding myself that it's a good thing that she can look back and laugh. If she had held on to the resentment, then she wouldn't still be here now. She'd be in an Uber, halfway home. Instead she's here with me, having agreed to takeout and a movie.

I can't complain.

I lay Rosie back in the crib. She sucks sweetly on her thumb, and her head lolls to the side. Within moments she's sleeping. I breathe a sigh of relief. As nice as it is spending the evening with my niece when she's quiet like this, I want to spend tonight with India.

She steps aside so that I can leave the room. We stand awkwardly on the landing for a moment before I usher her to follow me. I lead her through the house, to the living room. I see she's already picked out a film.

"*Saw*? Really?" I ask. She shrugs sheepishly.

"I was in the mood for a horror, I guess. Is that all right?"

Horror films are kind of my worst nightmare—

which I guess is entirely the point—but I want to keep India happy. I would literally watch a film about paint drying if it meant her sticking around for longer.

"Sure. Did you pick a takeout?"

"I thought pizza. A large with extra cheese and pepperoni. Side of garlic bread's a must," she says, scrolling through the menu with a serious expression on her face. I can't help but smile at her.

"I appreciate a woman with an appetite."

"Well, what can I say? A girl's got to eat."

"This is on me, so order what you want."

India looks like she's about to protest, but in the end she just nods and takes my credit card. "Thank you. I'm trying to save up money, so that would be a massive help."

"What are you saving for?"

India shrugs. "The future, I guess. I mean I adore my roommate, Montana, but I know one day she'll move on, and I'll want a place of my own. I could use a vacation too. It's been a while since I took any time off."

Come to think of it, India didn't take any time off while she was working for me the first time. I guess I never thought of it that much, but now I can see how seriously she took her job.

Come to think of it, I guess I've never had to worry about where the next paycheck is coming from. I've never had a debt that I didn't know for sure that I could pay, or had to worry about getting a mortgage. I've never scrimped on anything, not even when I was starting out. It just goes to show how different India's life really is to mine. And yet here we are, sitting side by side on my living room couch.

Too far apart to touch, but too close to think of anything else.

"You could really use a break. You work hard," I finally say.

India gives me a tired smile. "Yeah, well, after I finish up here, I'll be able to go anywhere, anytime. I can work remotely with the writing gig. I mean it's going well. I might travel for a while."

"Really? That's great." I nod at her, smiling. My chest constricts in a way I'm not sure I understand. Is it the thought of her leaving that makes me anxious? Or is it the fact that she's just too damn close for me to think straight at all?

"Yeah, just for a month or so. I'd love to go to Europe. See all the sights, work in a new environment, finish my novel."

"Sounds like you still plan to work. Not such a relaxing holiday after all."

India shrugs. "I like to keep busy. What about you? Wouldn't you like to see the world?"

She doesn't know she's struck a nerve, but she has. Once it was my dream to travel the globe. But it didn't work out. I ended up taking on work so demanding that I have no time to leave my company unattended for longer than a few days. Now it's simply a dream that I've packed away and for-gotten about.

"I guess someday I'll be able to pull away enough from my CEO duties to do that."

India doesn't look as though she believes me, but she lets it slide. She presses on the screen on her phone, looking pleased with herself.

"There. Pizza ordered. Shall we start the film?"

I nod, but even as on the movie starts, I know I won't pay attention to it at all. She's sitting so close to me that I can smell her shampoo. A fruity scent, strawberries and sugar. Her eyes are fixed on the screen, but I'm watching only her.

When the pizza arrives, I can barely eat, still more interested in what she's doing than food or some horror movie. By the time she's polished off half of the pizza and garlic bread, I've managed to eat only one slice.

"I thought you appreciated people with an ap-petite?" India says, glancing in my direction. On the screen, someone yells for help as they're being chased. I grimace.

"Yeah, I really do. I guess I'm just not hungry."

India cocks her head to the side. "Are you okay? You seem tense."

I swallow hard. It's a question I don't really want to answer, but I find myself responding before I can stop myself. "I'm always tense around you."

India's eyes widen, then her face slowly relaxes into a smile. I hadn't noticed, but she's moved even closer. Her arm is draped around the back of the sofa. Her other hand moves to graze my leg.

"Good," she says quietly. Then a silence falls over us. I can hear my own breathing. India traces her fingers up my leg and I try not to groan. Her touch is electric. She leans forward slowly.

She's going to kiss me. She's going to kiss me.

Rosie chooses the perfect moment to start crying. The baby monitor crackles and then she starts to wail. India jerks, drawing back from me, her cheeks a little flushed. I swallow, standing up.

"I need to go and check on her."

India waves me away with a flick of her hand. "Sure, yeah. Absolutely."

Feeling more than a little frustrated, I bound up the stairs. Part of me hopes that Rosie will quiet down quickly so that I can get back to India, but I guess the mood has already passed. I want to cry out in frustration. We were so close. How did this happen?

When I reach Rosie, there's an unmistakably bad smell. I groan. Operation diaper change is in order. I sigh, picking Rosie up and holding her at arm's length for a moment. I shake my head at her.

"I knew tonight was too good to be true, you little monkey."

Rosie continues screaming, but I swear there's also a mischievous glint in her eye.

Thirteen

India

*D*amn.

That's all I can think. Damn it. Damn the interruption that stopped us from hooking up. I almost can't believe it. We got so close, and then just like that the flame was extinguished.

I'm so embarrassed that I was so bold. What is he thinking? That I'm some psycho secretary out to seduce my boss?

No, but see, that's the thing. It didn't feel like he was my boss just now, that I worked for him. It just felt like a night with a guy I like. A guy who makes my heart beat faster and my body tingle.

He's still upstairs, tending to Rosie. I'm sitting alone in his living room, wringing my hands, half watching the film and half trying to figure out what's going on in my head. I wonder if he was glad he had an excuse to walk away, or if he wanted it to happen as much as I did. Couldn't he have just indulged me for a few moments if he was actually interested? Was it really so urgent that he had to leave right away?

At this point I just want to go home, but I don't want things to be awkward come Monday. Leaving now would make it seem like I'm freaked out by this whole thing, which I totally am, but he can't know that. I need to act like nothing went on and pretend that I never tried to kiss my boss.

God, what was I thinking? Even if he is interested, there's so much that could go wrong, just from a simple kiss.

But I still want to take the risk.

The baby monitor goes quiet after a while and I hear William coming back down the stairs. He stealthily reenters the room, flopping down on the sofa next to me.

"She's a little rascal, that girl," he says, his gaze on the TV screen. I can tell he's nervous. He's sitting farther away than before, and his posture is stiff. It only makes me think more that he didn't want to kiss me. I try for a smile, but I'm struggling to hide my disappointment. William clears his throat. He's obviously feeling the pressure as much as I am.

"Would you like a drink? I mean, it *is* the weekend…"

I breathe a sigh of relief. A drink would be great right now. "Sure."

"Gin and tonic?"

"Perfect."

William disappears for a few minutes and I try to use the time to pull myself together. *Stop being pathetic,* I tell myself. *Just be grateful Rosie interrupted before you could do something stupid.*

William returns with my drink and I dive right in, draining half the glass in one go. William looks a little surprised, but he doesn't say anything. The film ends and William absentmindedly puts another on, though I can tell that neither of us is interested in watching it. We both finish our first drinks and he pours us another. Then another. I'm beginning to feel confident again. I check him out, staring at his chiseled abs pushing against the fabric his shirt. Then I let my eyes rest on the faint line of stubble on his chin. I check out his bare arms, the veins on them prominent against his tanned skin.

I want him.

I look up and am jolted when I realize he's looking at me too. Our eyes lock and we watch each other for a moment. I can barely breathe. I want to touch him, but I don't want to make the first move. Especially since it went so poorly for me last time. No. If he wants this, he can move first.

He's tentative. I knew he would be, if he made a

move at all. But he's inching closer. He reaches for my chin, holding my face in place. The gesture takes my breath away. Our eyes meet. He looks serious, but impassioned.

"What game are you playing with me, India?" he asks, fiercely.

I breathe a little faster.

I don't reply for a long moment. William searches my face, his gaze intense.

"Kiss me," I suddenly breathe, just blurting it out.

I don't know where that comes from.

It comes from somewhere very hidden, somewhere I never care to visit. But it's out in the open now. William's blue eyes flare and my lips part as the full realization of what I just asked of him hits me.

He narrows his eyes as his gaze dips to my mouth. Cursing softly, he shifts his hold on me and drives his fingers into the fall of my hair behind my head. He leans closer and pulls me forward at the same time with one quick, strong jerk.

And just like that, our lips crash together. Just like that, William crushes my mouth beneath his.

I close my eyes. I can taste the gin he's been drinking and feel the buzz run through me. His tongue touches mine and I groan into him, clawing at his shoulders for more. His breath is hot. His skin is hotter.

He's kissing me like he's dying for it.

I'm kissing him back like it's the only chance I'll ever get.

But suddenly it's not enough.

I want everything. Every piece of him.

I take the reins. I awkwardly clamber on top of him, positioning myself over his crotch and grinding against him as I grab fistfuls of his hair and keep on kissing him. He's clearly not used to this—I can feel his heartbeat as I caress his chest with my free hand. He's more excited than I am, if that's possible.

He groans low and deep against my mouth as I grind harder against him. I like that he's vocal—it's good to know when you're turning a man on. I let my hand run down his chest, feeling every single muscle there as I move to unzip his pants.

I want him too much to even bother with foreplay.

And that's the moment that he stops me.

His lips are gone from mine in an instant, leaving me with a cold and hollow feeling in my chest. We were barely getting started, and he wants to end it? I know logic dictates that we should, but has the relationship between William and me ever been logical or straightforward? Absolutely not. So why, all of a sudden, is he concerned about breaking a few rules?

William pushes me away a couple of inches, shaking his head vehemently, his jaw clenched so hard that a muscle twitches in his cheek. "God, India, I'm sorry. I shouldn't have let this happen. This was such a bad idea."

"A good-bad idea," I insist, moving to kiss his neck. He doesn't push me away this time, but he does groan, partly from desire, partly from frustration, as though I'm an irritating child. Maybe that's how he sees me most of the time.

"Look, this is highly unprofessional of me…" He clutches my shoulders in his big hands again.

God, but he's so hard, I'm weak everywhere just feeling him beneath me.

"So what? You're never going to win a boss-of-the-year award. At least this is more fun than you shouting at me or whatever," I argue, diving to taste the raspy skin on his jaw.

William pushes me off more firmly this time and sets me on my feet. Gasping as he peels me away, I look down at him. He's breathing hard. I can see him waging a war inside. His erection is visible through his pants, but he quickly covers himself with a cushion.

"Come on, India. You know this is a terrible idea. You're my assistant." He drags a hand down his face. He's flushed, and his eyes are such a brilliant blue, they're like lasers.

"Not for much longer," I say quietly, my heart pounding so hard I'm trembling. "And we're not in the office… Technically I'm not even on work time. This doesn't have to be a huge thing. Besides, who is going to know?"

He's watching me hungrily. I can tell he's close to giving in to me. When a man is so starved of sex, it doesn't take much, of course. Just a little more of a push and I can have him in the palm of my hand.

And William is a workaholic.

He hasn't even gone on dates since I started working for him. I can always tell by his schedule; I've been the one keeping it all this time. I know he wants it. He's starved for it. I can find a way to get him to do anything I ask. I want to cajole, beg, plead. But before I can vamp up the seduction, he stands up, shaking his head.

"No one else would know, but I would, India," he says sternly, straightening his shirt. "My job is everything. I've seen what this kind of thing can cause. My brother got into a massive amount of trouble for sleeping with an employee. She had to quit her job to save his, in the end. They resolved it, true, but it wasn't easy. I'm not going to jeopardize my reputation for…a hookup."

The comment stings. I mean, I was never expecting marriage and kids after what happens tonight, but somehow it hurts to be regarded simply as a hookup. Do the memories we've shared this week mean nothing to him? After everything, are we still at the same sad place where we began?

I don't want to give up because somewhere in his eyes, I see a gleam of need that calls to me, that tells me he wants this as badly as I do, but I don't want to beg. At the same time… I can't just leave it like this.

I'm too tipsy, my emotions too much on the surface. And I can tell William is too close to breaking his steely resolve for me to back out.

We stand in silence for a few moments. Then, before I can change my mind, I slowly move my hand to the first button on my shirt. I pop it open with nimble fingers. Then another. Then another. William stares at me, transfixed, as slowly my shirt opens up.

He swallows once.

Then twice.

His voice is thick and raspy. "What are you doing?"

I don't respond. I wonder if he might try to stop me. For the sake of "professionalism." He doesn't. He's too stunned at first, and then he's simply gaping. He can't bring himself to actively touch me or respond to my body, but he's watching, for sure.

Dizzy with desire and high on my own effect on him—and his effect on me—as I see the unmistakable gleam of desire in his eyes, I pop open the last button and my shirt falls away, revealing my bra. I shrug the shirt off, letting it drop to the floor in a heap. William's eyes flicker between me and the shirt like he can't quite believe what's happening.

I unzip my pants, stepping gracefully out of them. I'm just in my underwear now. I knew there was a good reason to wear a thong today. William's eyes eat me up, but I wish he'd do something. *Grab me*, I want to tell him. *Do something*.

I flick my hair back over my shoulders. This little striptease has gotten me hot and bothered. I run a hand through my hair and over my neck. I stop for a moment to cup my own breast, moving the bra's material aside to pinch my nipple. William's intake of breath matches the gasp that I let out. It feels good, but I wish it was William touching me like this. I need to step up my game to entice him.

I never remember wanting a man in this way. Needing his touch like I need his.

Shaking with adrenaline, I perch myself on his coffee table. I can see that he's anxious to see what I do next.

Too hot to be shy, I spread my legs apart, amazed at my own boldness. I know what will rile him up. I know what will convince him to break his word.

My hand slides inside my underwear. William's eyes widen. I gasp at the shock of feeling his blue eyes run all over my near-naked form. Then I run my tongue across my lips in a way I hope comes out as seductive rather than nervous. Now I have his attention. My fingers delve into my wetness, exploring my most sensitive area. William stands very still, his eyes focused on the movements of my fingers. I remove them from my panties for a moment. Why isn't he doing anything? Why isn't he grabbing me right now?

I stand up and head across the room, and as he watches me approach, William starts to lower himself to the couch.

Is he sitting because he wanted to get away from me and bumped into the couch? Or because he can't stand straight because of me?

Suddenly it doesn't matter, and I'm straddling him again. He doesn't stop me. He's breathing hard. His hands sliding possessively down my back, cupping my bottom and squeezing as if both to edge me away and pull me closer. I lift my wet fingers up to his lips and his tongue emerges to lick them. I moan softly. Finally. He's finally getting into this.

I lean closer, brushing his lips with mine. His hands clench on my ass even harder, his erection pulsing against the V-shape of my legs.

"India," he rasps.

I'm shivering for him. But I can't just hand him everything. He needs to do some work too.

With gargantuan effort, I stand up, moving slowly away from him. He looks confused as I gather up my clothes. I raise an eyebrow at him, and he blinks as if to clear the fog of alcohol and me.

"If you want this," I whisper, "then you'll find me in the spare bedroom."

When he doesn't respond, I force myself to walk away. I move slowly, hoping that William might try to catch me up and sweep me off my feet. But as I ascend the stairs, there's no sign of him. I wonder what the hell he's waiting for. I couldn't have made myself any clearer.

Doesn't he want this?

I let myself into the spare room and arrange myself on the bed. I'm so wet with anticipation that I long to touch myself, but I force myself to wait. I want him to be the one to bring me to a climax. I want him to be the reason my legs are trembling with anticipation. But there's no sign of him.

I wait. I keep waiting for him to burst through the

door and take me. But as the alcohol slowly leaves my system, I begin to sober to the idea that he's not coming. I did everything to make that man interested, and he's left me alone with not a shred of dignity left.

As I feel myself drifting off to sleep, the effect of alcohol and nerves too much for me, I ask myself, *What have I done?*

Fourteen

William

What have I done?

I've really fucked this one up. I had one chance to sleep with the woman of my dreams. One chance to prove to her—and myself—that I'm not a waste of time. That I'm worth investing in. She gave me everything I could possibly ask for. She gave me a striptease, for God's sake. She was sexy, enchanting and naughty as hell…and I passed up the chance to be a part of it.

Why didn't I follow her to the spare room? Why did I just sit there while she touched herself, smiling at me like she knew exactly what she wanted from me? Why didn't I give her everything she's ever yearned for?

Because I'm a fucking idiot, that's why.

Too uptight.

I was so caught up in my own fears. Fears of being controversial. Fears of stepping over a line that I have created for myself, penning me in with my own rules and insecurities. I managed to convince myself that I was doing the right thing when I watched her walk away and didn't follow. But after an hour had passed, and she still hadn't come back to the living room, I went in to check on her and she was sound asleep. I'd completely blown my chance with her.

And now I've woken up, alone in my bed with a screaming baby for company. India is alone in the spare bedroom, neglected and surely unsatisfied.

We could have both been winners last night if only I wasn't such a loser.

I get up as quickly as I can, though the room is spinning. One too many gin and tonics, clearly. I tend to Rosie, who to her credit quietens down as soon as she's changed and fed. Then I decide I need to find India. That is, if she hasn't already left. I need to apologize and straighten things out before I dig myself into a deeper hole.

When I head to the spare room, the door is open and the bed is made. No sign of India. I shake my head, running downstairs to see if I can find her. The remnants of our movie night are scattered across the living room. There's popcorn on the floor and the

pizza box is strewn on one of the chairs. Half-full
gin glasses litter the table where I watched India
touch herself. Just the thought of it makes me hard,
but I can't give in to my emotions right now. I need
to figure out where she is.

I hear the coffee machine in the kitchen firing up
and head there. India is standing in yesterday's suit,
making herself a large coffee. She glances around
as I enter, but quickly looks away again. I may have
imagined it, but I'm sure I saw the ghost of a blush
on her freckled cheeks.

"India…"

"Good morning, Mr. Walker. I can't believe I'm
still here this morning, but it's fine. As soon as I have
my coffee, I'll take a car home."

"Really? You're just going to pretend like nothing happened."

India whips around with fire in her eyes, though
she keeps her face calm. She sips her coffee, glar-
ing in my direction.

"Well, you did a pretty good job of pretending
nothing was happening *while* it was happening last
night," India says. "So let's just forget the whole
thing, shall we?"

"Look, I'm sorry—"

"No," India cuts me off. "I made a mistake. I made
a mistake in thinking you were interested. I made a
mistake in thinking you were…different. But I was
wrong on both counts. So you can drop it right now,
and I'll be on my way."

"India—"

"Please."

She raises her eyes to me then, and the pain I see there stuns me. Silences me. Punches me in the damn gut and makes me feel like the worst man in the entire world.

"India," I repeat, swallowing as I raise my hand to touch her. But we're interrupted by a loud knock on the door. I frown. Who could it be on a Saturday morning? India raises an eyebrow at me.

"Are you getting that, Mr. Walker, or do you want me to?"

I grit my molars. I know she's refusing to call me William to piss me off. It's certainly working. I head for the door, frustrated and not even interested about who might be on the other side. I open it and blink in surprise.

"Dad? What are you doing here?"

My father is standing at the door, holding a large pink plush bunny rabbit. He's clearly here for Rosie rather than me.

"Do I need an excuse to visit my son and granddaughter?" he asks, glancing around as though Rosie might materialize at any moment. "Where is the little angel?"

"In my room. Asleep."

"Ah, well then. I suppose you can make me a coffee while she's resting."

I awkwardly allow my father to step inside, wondering how I'm going to explain my assistant's being here in an absolutely foul mood. He heads straight for the living room and finds the mess of last night. He smiles.

"Have you had company? Or has little Rosie been trying out her first gin and tonics?" he asks, tapping one of the glasses with a wiggle of his eyebrows. I'm about to explain when India makes her appearance, looking completely unimpressed.

"You remember my father, Alistair Walker?" I quickly say.

She nods briefly to my father.

"Morning, Mr. Walker," she says. She's met him a few times before at work functions. Dad looks back and forth between the two of us with a questioning expression.

"Morning, India. Is there a reason you're here so early on a Saturday morning?"

"I was just leaving," India says curtly. She's not the kind to make excuses, so my father's imagination is likely running wild.

"Well, no hurry, my dear! I just came to check in on my son and Rosie. Have they both been good?"

India cocks her head to the side. "Funnily enough, I'd say your son is more childish than the baby. I'm sure you know that already, though."

Dad laughs loudly, clapping a hand on my back. "Son, I like this young lady. Though she doesn't seem to like *you*, clearly." He looks back at India. "See, my son needs a good woman to keep him on his toes. Keep his perspective in check, you know?"

India nods, her expression blank. "Sure. I'll be sure to give out his number if I ever meet one keen enough to take him on."

I can't help being angry at the pair of them, teasing me as though I'm not here. It makes me feel three inches tall. I want to snap back, tell my father what India is really bitter about, but I keep my mouth shut. Shoving my hands angrily into my slack pockets.

"Well, India, I guess you're right and he could use a little help in finding a woman like that. You're his assistant, right? Why not *assist* in setting him up? Do you know anyone who he might click with?"

"Not really. But does your son even know what it is that he wants?"

Another dig. I wish she'd leave already, but I have a feeling my father isn't going to let this one go. He's enjoying himself far too much to give up now.

"Well, let's be honest, at this point he'll have any woman who'll take him, eh, son?" he jests, nudging me in the ribs. India cracks a smug smile.

"Well... I guess I do know someone I could convince to go on a date. She's single, pretty, well mannered, career-driven... And she has the patience of a saint. She's going to need it."

Dad claps his hands together. "Excellent! Give me her info and we'll set something up for later this week. I can babysit while he heads out on his date. William will take your friend out to a lovely restaurant. When is your last day, India? Next Friday?

Maybe that would be the perfect night for a date to take his mind off his losses."

India glances at me, her eyes still blazing with a little anger. "I'm sure that can be arranged."

"That's enough, both of—"

"Nonsense, son. Lighten up. We're just having a bit of fun. Still, you have to admit you need to put yourself out there more."

"Dad—"

Before I can argue further, there's more commotion at the front door. This time it's Henry, who lets himself in with his spare key.

"The car's ready now," he says politely, unaware of the strange conversation he's interrupted. "I'd be happy to take Ms. Crowley home."

"Thank you, Henry," I say, glancing at her. India looks back at me, unsuccessful at hiding another blush as our eyes meet, despite the fact that she obviously hates me. "See you on Monday, Mr. Walker."

The pair leave together in silence. The moment the door closes behind them, Dad chuckles to himself.

"Well, son. Things were a little frosty just then, wouldn't you say?"

I shake my head at him. "I can't believe you."

"Oh, please. Can't you take a joke? Besides, maybe you do need to go out on a blind date to loosen up."

I throw my hands up in exasperation.

"What? Maybe you've already got someone else in mind?" Dad says with faux curiosity. I can tell he sees right through me.

"Dad—"

"I thought so. Your problem is that you sit around and wait until it's too late. You need to put in the work. Flirt a little."

"And you're seriously encouraging me to go for it with my *assistant*?"

"Look, you know I'm not the kind of man who cares about that. I gave Alex and Kit my blessing, didn't I?"

"Yes, but after you gave them hell first."

"Oh, blast that. And aren't they happy now, after taking so many risks to be together?"

"Well, yes, but—"

"Stop making excuses for yourself, William. Just let it happen. Go with the flow for once, for Christ's sake. You never know—you might actually have something worth fighting for here." He nudges me gently. "Besides, doesn't she leave her position in a week? After that she's fair game."

He could be right. He usually is. But will she ever forgive me for the way I left her alone last night?

Have I screwed this up entirely, or will I get another chance?

One thing I know about India is that she's got walls up even higher than mine.

Fifteen

India

One more week. Just one more week. That's how much longer I have to spend with the insufferable William Walker. Then I'll be able to walk out and never see him again, with a healthy sum of money in my back pocket.

So why does the prospect of leaving disappoint me so much?

After the way he humiliated me, it's almost un-bearable to think about going back to his house. Yet here I am, preparing to head for work, back to the scene of the crime. And a part of me is actually desperate to get back there. Why? I have no clue.

Maybe some sick part of me is hoping he might have changed his mind again. He clearly flits from decision to decision the way his brother used to flit from woman to woman. He doesn't know his own mind. But I can't be the one to teach him how to think for himself. It's too big of a task to take on over the space of a week, and by then I'll be gone.

I just have to accept that the whole thing between us was a massive mistake. No matter how much he begs or tries to persuade me otherwise, I have to make sure that this is the end. Because I'm the one who gets hurt each time we get closer. If only to protect myself, I have to keep my distance from William.

I'm an only child who never really felt like I lived up to my parents' expectations of me. A close family like the one William has is something I've always craved. Yes. Seeing him with his niece sort of melts my heart. And yes, talking to him and seeing this whole other side to him has an effect too.

But his rejection stung in more ways than one. It made me feel, once again, as if I'm not good enough. I hate feeling like this. Especially when a part of me just wants him to think well of me because I've started to think more than well of *him*.

I go to the kitchen to make some breakfast. It's still super early, but to my surprise Montana is waiting for me in the kitchen. I try for a smile, though I feel like breaking down in tears. Montana isn't convinced by my attempts at all.

"Morning," I say quietly, avoiding her gaze. She folds her arms.

"Are you going to tell me what happened on Saturday? Or are you just going to keep pretending like everything is fine?"

I shake my head as I open the fridge. "There's nothing to say." I can't imagine telling Montana about this one. What would I say? That I did a strip-tease for my boss and then got upset when he didn't take an interest.

Pathetic. I'm truly *pathetic*.

But Montana isn't one to give up. "You don't owe that man anything, Indy. You could walk away right now. Forget the money—it's not important. If you think working there for another week is going to make you this miserable, you should quit while you're ahead."

"I'm fine."

"You're *not*. I know you better than anyone. I can see when you're upset. I can tell that he did something to upset you."

"So, what's new? He's my boss. He's not here to baby me and make me feel good about myself."

"India, look—"

"Just leave it, Montana," I plead. "I can handle myself. I know what I'm doing, okay? You just need to trust that I'm strong enough to know my limits. If it gets to be too much, I'll quit. I promise."

Montana sighs, staring at her hands. "The trouble is, India, I think you believe you're made of stone.

Just like him. And you're not. There's clearly more to this than you're letting on, and you're going to end up with more pain than you bargained for. I don't want to see that happen."

I take a deep breath. What does Montana know about how strong I can be? And how can she possibly sense that there's more to this? I haven't told her how much he's come to mean to me. I haven't told her how I feel. But maybe I don't need to.

Is it that obvious to everyone that I'm falling for the wrong man?

I cross my arms defensively. "Look, you don't need to worry. Everything is going to be okay."

Montana stares at me for a moment, like she's trying to figure out who the person in front of her is. Then she stands up and grabs her water bottle from the counter. "If that's what you believe. But just be careful. I don't want to have to watch you crumble."

As she leaves, I feel my heart sink. She's right about everything. I'm out of my depth with William Walker. But he doesn't need to know that he's got me in a mess. I'm not going to let him see the effect he's had. I set my face into a hardened expression. I lift my chin up.

I convince myself I'm fine, even if no one else is fooled but me.

The ride to work seems to take forever, but forever doesn't last long enough. As we pull up in front of William's house, I'm almost consumed by dread.

I take a deep breath, hoping that no one will notice that my hands are shaking. I have to take this one step at a time. Minute by minute. Hour by hour. Day by day. I'm so close to being rid of William forever. I'm not going to back out of this for anything.

Henry gives me a sympathetic look as he turns the car around and drives off, probably to run some errands. I blush hard. Maybe he's noticed the tension too. But I can't let myself fall apart and fulfill everyone's expectations. I have to play this cool. I opt to knock on the front door so that I don't wake Rosie. It takes a few minutes, but soon enough William shows up, holding Rosie against his chest. He looks tired. Tired, but beautiful.

He almost looks shocked to see me, as though he'd forgotten I work here now. Either that or he was hoping he'd broken me down enough to scare me off. Well, hah. Thought you'd seen the last of me, William? Not a chance.

"India…good morning."

I nod curtly to him, before raising an eyebrow. He's standing in my way. He hastily moves out of my path and I enter the house, keeping my shoulders square as I do. I have to ooze confidence, as though I'm the dominant one here. I have to look the part, even if I don't feel it. Perhaps I'm a better actress than I think, because all of a sudden William is stumbling over his words, trying to say something.

"Listen, India… I mean, the weekend…well, I just think—"

I hold up my hand to silence him. "I don't want to hear another word," I say quietly. "I'm not interested in what you've got to say on the matter." I focus on Rosie. "Hello, gorgeous princess."

She grins at me, and I cup her hair and give her a smile too.

"Not even if I'm trying to say I'm sorry?" William sounds frustrated, forcing me to glance back up at him.

That's not what I was expecting. I was expecting excuses, defense strategies, battle talk. Anything to protect his own skin. But here he is, actually prepared to take the blame for what happened over the weekend. Am I really going to shut him down before he says anything?

William seems to take my shocked silence as a good thing. He adjusts Rosie in his arms. "Look…if you just give me ten minutes to get Rosie settled, we can sit down and talk properly. Except for a couple of conference calls, my schedule is relatively free today."

"I'm so glad you can find time for me in your *busy schedule*," I say, trying for a mocking tone. But my heart isn't really in it. I want to hear him out, even though I promised myself I wouldn't give him any leeway. This is a dangerous path for me to take. He might start thinking he can get away with anything, the way he used to. But it's so tempting that I just nod.

William exhales audibly, then nods in return,

rocking Rosie gently as he heads for the stairs. He's speaking softly to the baby, and it warms my heart. I wish it didn't. I don't want to trust him or think of him as anything but my nightmare boss. Otherwise this all becomes too hard.

I move through to the living room and sit down, trying to compose myself for this conversation. Part of me knows, though, that I'm totally unprepared for it.

When William returns, I'm as ready as I'll ever be. He sits on the couch, but as far from me as possible. Maybe he's scared of how I might react to this conversation. If he knew anything at all, he'd know I'm all bark and no bite. He'd know that I feel just as vulnerable as he does right now.

William takes a deep breath, raking a hand through his hair. "Okay. So… I guess I should start by saying I'm sorry, again."

I stare at his throat, unable to meet his gaze. Forcing my voice to sound level, I ask, "About which part?"

"For leaving you alone like that. After you…after you did what you did… I wanted to follow you. I did. But I had some concerns."

"Concerns about what? Human contact?"

There's dead silence.

I lift my gaze, wanting to cry as our eyes meet. William is giving me a pleading, totally helpless look. "India, come on. Are you really going to make me spell it out for you like this?"

I swallow, forcing myself to hold his gaze. I want him to know that's exactly what I'm expecting him to do. He sighs, moving his thumb to his lips. He nibbles at his skin, avoiding eye contact.

"Okay… I was concerned about the consequences. Concerned about how it might affect our work together. Concerned that I wouldn't be good enough for you. Concerned that if I slept with a woman so beautiful, so funny, so intelligent…that it would have a more permanent effect on me than anything ever has."

I almost feel sympathetic, but then I remember that the Walker boys are masters of wordplay. He probably has me exactly where he wants me. I fold my arms, shaking my head. "No. Don't feed me that bullshit."

"I swear, India, it's not a line. I… I guess I'm scared of messing things up before they even get started."

"I was looking for a one-night stand, not a marriage proposal."

William blushes. "I understand. But that's complicated in itself. You're my employee…"

"Just barely."

"Right. But still, you work for me for the time being. Sex can…complicate things. These past two weeks have been complex enough. Don't you see that adding something else to the equation makes this entire scenario even crazier?"

I roll my eyes. "Trust you to overcomplicate everything. Why does it have to mean more than what it is on paper?"

William gives me a knowing look. "After your response to this, I think we both know we couldn't pass it off as meaningless."

He's so annoyingly right. I don't want to admit it, but he's completely spot-on—I can't have a meaningless experience with William. Someone's feelings will get hurt. This whole time, I was expecting that I was the one who would suffer most. But what if William's feelings are as strong as mine?

What if William is scared too?

He shuffles a little closer to me on the couch and my heart leaps in my chest. He looks down at his lap as he works up the courage to speak. "I'm not saying that any of this would be a good idea," he begins carefully. "But…maybe instead of diving in the deep end, we could…just spend some time together?"

"You think that after everything you've put me through that I want to spend *more* time with you? More time being humiliated?"

William glances up at me. A ghost of a smile plays on his lips and he suddenly looks so gorgeous and boyish and mesmerizing that it's almost scary. "I think that despite it all, you do. You want to be around me. You want to explore these feelings. I can see it in your eyes."

I resist the urge to cover my face. I'm sick of my expressions giving me away. Because he's right. Even after everything, I want to stay here, with him.

He's looking at me. He's waiting for a reaction. I want to lean forward and kiss him, but if I did, it would feel like I was betraying myself. I can't give in easily to him just because he's made some kind of apology.

I clear my throat. "Here's how this is going to work. You're going to get one chance, and one chance only. We can spend this evening together. No touching, just talking. We can see how it goes. And then we'll take it from there. But I swear, you'd better come up with something good. I'm not sticking around if you're going to cause me more problems."

William allows himself to smile, finally. "Don't worry, India. I'm not planning on messing up my final chance with you."

Sixteen

William

When Rosie starts crying at 10:00 a.m., I couldn't be more relieved. The atmosphere in my office has been tense since India and I relocated there today. She's not said much since our earlier conversation, and I don't blame her. After the debacle on Friday night, she has every right to be wary of me. But I'm determined to prove to her that she's not making a mistake by giving me one last chance.

I have to get this right. That's the one thought that keeps running through my head. I'm keenly aware of it each time I look at her. To me, she seems out of my league. She's too good for me in every single way, and I have to make tonight count. I have to step up and prove that I'm the man she wants me to be.

The problem is how can I prove to her that I like her? I'm not really a romantic. I'm not known for my sense of humor or for being a great conversationalist. In fact, she just knows me as her nightmare boss. I want her to see me as I am—reserved but caring. A little misunderstood, perhaps, but willing to change. I want her to see that I'm not always going to be some guy who lets her down. There's a lot of pressure, though, and only one more opportunity to get this right. So much rides on this, and I don't have a clue how to approach the scenario.

It takes me almost an hour to get Rosie settled, and when I return to the office, India pays very little attention to my presence. I sit down at my desk, clearing my throat to see if she'll respond. When she doesn't, I sigh and try to focus on my work, but thoughts of the evening we will share fill my mind. I still haven't come up with anything for us to do.

I watch her from the corner of my eye. She's typing furiously on her laptop, engrossed in her writing. Like me, she's constantly immersed in her work. So maybe I need to do something to help her relax. Something to get out of the work mind-set. Give her an escape.

And suddenly I have a perfect idea.

I stand up slowly, trying not to distract India from her work. If she asks where I'm going, I'll probably stumble over my words. I'm a terrible liar. But she

doesn't even glance my way, so I leave the room un-
noticed. I sneak down the corridor, take out my cell
and call Henry. He picks up right away.

"Can I help you, sir?"

"Yes, you can, actually. But I have a bit of a strange
request."

Henry is quiet on the other end of the line. I guess
his mind is running through a thousand possibilities.
I think my request is likely to set his thoughts racing even more. I check that India hasn't followed me,
before lowering my voice even further.

"I need you to get me a women's swimsuit."

The end of the workday approaches, and I'm anx-
iously waiting for Henry to return from his mission.
I can't imagine what he thinks. I'm sure he's figured
out that something is happening with India. Hopefully he's brought me something she'll like.

He texts me just as four o'clock approaches. India
glances at me as I stand up, hoping to sneak off and
get her swimsuit.

"What's with you being all shifty? You've been
fidgeting all day."

So, she did notice. Maybe I'm not as subtle as I
thought. I struggle for an excuse. "I'm just going to
check on Rosie," I lie, impressed with my own abil-
ity to cover my tracks. India shrugs.

"Okay. I'll pack up."

I slip from the room and hurry downstairs. I don't
want India figuring out I lied to her. That's the last

thing I need right now, even if I did it for the sake of our evening. I want it to be special. I quietly open the front door and there Henry is, waiting for me on the front step. I raise an eyebrow at him.

"Well? Did you get something?"

Henry's face is bright red. "I did… The shop assistant recommended it to me. I described India and she thought this would be perfect."

I nod enthusiastically. At least I know Henry has some sense. "Can I see it?"

Henry blushes a darker shade. "I'm… Okay. I hope it's okay."

He hands me a fancy-looking bag and I open it to see what's inside. Then I slowly remove the swimsuit, staring at it in horror. It looks a little like a spider's web—the black material is woven from thin, spindly pieces of fabric that look like they won't cover much at all. I look at the price tag. It's described as a thong swimsuit.

I drop it back into the bag. "Are you crazy? Buying my assistant this? She's going to think I want her dressed like a porn star or something!"

Henry frowns. "Well, I'm sorry, but you didn't give me much information to work with. And I thought the point was for it to be sexy? I assumed…"

I shake my head. This is a disaster. She's going to be so mad when she sees this stupid swimsuit. I rub my face, suddenly completely exhausted. "All right, Henry. Thank you for trying."

"Are you keeping it?"

"Keeping what?"

Henry and I both jump and turn. India is standing on the stairs, peering to see what's in the bag. I sigh, holding out the bag to her in resignation.

"I... I thought we could try out the hot tub tonight. Watch the sunset."

She ignores me, descending the stairs to take the bag. She peers inside and I hold my breath, preparing for her to walk straight out the door. But I watch her expression turn from confusion to an amused smirk. She rolls her eyes to herself, tutting. Then she glances up to meet my gaze with a wicked smile.

"I'll meet you up there," she says. Then she turns on her heel and heads for the bathroom.

That woman never ceases to surprise me.

Henry breathes a sigh of relief, patting me on the back.

"You dodged a bullet there, boss. Good luck with the rest of the evening..."

Henry makes a quick escape, and I don't blame him. This whole evening feels like it could burst into flames at any moment.

But I guess that's part of the fun.

It's getting dark quickly. On fall nights in Chicago, the sunsets can be particularly beautiful, and I'm looking forward to tonight's. I sit in the hot tub with a bottle of prosecco on ice beside me, hoping that India will hurry up. I don't want her to miss this.

But when she steps outside, I forget the sunset

for a moment. She's wearing the swimsuit with confidence. Her curls cascade down her back, but the
skin there is bare otherwise. The swimsuit dips at
the front, revealing her full breasts. Her hips are
bare too, and I discover that she has a small tattoo
of a heart on her hip. She sashays toward the hot
tub, locking eyes with me as she does. I know it's a
game she's playing with me—she wants to know if
I'll continue looking at her body. Of course I want
to, but I want to stay in her good books more. I keep
my eyes on hers, smiling gently.

"Hop in. It's nice and warm."

"Well, they don't call it a hot tub for nothing," she
says, but without a hint of sass. She's just teasing. I
immediately move to pour her a glass of prosecco,
but she shakes her head.

"Not on a work night," she says. "That didn't work
out so well for me last time, if you remember."

I assume she's referring to the night before she
quit. That seems like such a long time ago now,
though it's been less than two weeks. Yet so much
has changed. If someone told me I'd be in a hot tub
with my assistant a week back, I would've called
them crazy. Now she's delicately stepping into the
bubbling water, dressed in a revealing swimsuit, with
a smile on her face. It's almost like a dream, but
when I pinch myself slyly under the water, I know
it's real.

She sighs as she settles into the water. She tips

her head back and closes her eyes. I watch the stray strands of her hair floating in the water.

"I needed this," she says.

I clear my throat. "That's why I thought...yeah, I thought you'd enjoy it. I'm... I'm sorry about the swimsuit. I wasn't expecting Henry to come back with...well, that."

She smiles to herself, her eyes still closed. "You worry a lot, don't you?"

I frown at that. I'm glad she hasn't opened her eyes. I don't want her to know how easily she can get to me. "I guess so. I'm working on that though."

India nods, finally opening her eyes again. "Me too. I guess going with the flow isn't so bad, right? Not everything has to be planned down to a tee."

I nod, though I think we both disagree with that statement on some level. We thrive on perfectly laid-out plans. But at this moment, in a hot tub with my assistant, I guess that philosophy has gone straight out the window.

"It's like writing a novel," India continues. "I always thought that if I could get an outline down on paper, then everything would go smoothly from there. I mean how far wrong can you go when you've basically got step-by-step instructions in front of you? But I guess it doesn't ever happen that way. Life gets in the way. New ideas. Things change and all that."

I nod. She could say anything right now and I would probably agree. I lap up her words easily.

She seems to make so much sense, even though I'm hardly listening to the actual words she's saying.

The sunset is beginning. The sky is the color of autumn leaves. India watches quietly, thoughtfully. I wonder what's on her mind. Is she thinking about me, the way I'm thinking about her?

She cocks her head to the side, glancing in my direction. "Funnily enough, I've never watched the sunset that closely. I've described it a thousand times. As writers do so often. But I've never watched one." She smiles, and it relaxes me a little. She doesn't look angry at me, for once. It makes a nice change, for sure. "Thanks for this. This was a good idea."

"So…are we okay?"

"Maybe don't push it," she says, but there's a twinkle in her eyes that tells me she's only kidding. I breathe a sigh of relief. I'm back in her good books, at least temporarily. Now all I need to do is get through the rest of the evening without messing up. I clear my throat. This is my chance to delve a little deeper and get to know her better.

"So, your writing…do you write about real life?"

She lets out a contented sigh, shifting in the water. "Most of the time. I'm not really a fantasy type of girl. I get the appeal—an escape from the real world, I guess. But for me, I'd rather write about something real. Something everyone can relate to and experience."

"So, romance?"

She shrugs. "Not necessarily. But sometimes, yes.

I like to write about life as people live it. Real people, real lives. Simple lives."

I know what she's getting at. She's saying she wouldn't write about people like me. The types of people who are so high in the clouds that they've forgotten what it's like to have their feet on solid ground. Is it a dig at me, I wonder, or does she really just like to keep things simple?

She seems to realize how I might take her words and bites her lip. "I'm not judging you at all. I just don't think many people would understand the kind of life you live. I mean, come on. Sunsets and champagne on the roof. That's the kind of thing most of us might experience once on an expensive holiday. Not on a random Monday night after work."

I frown. "So you're saying I'm spoiled?"

She laughs. It's a nice laugh—loud, but not abrasive or forced. "No, not at all…though if the shoe fits."

I smile, splashing her a little. She laughs again, sending a tidal wave of water my way in return. I splutter as the water hits my face and I hold my hands up in surrender.

"All right, all right," I say, chuckling. She raises a triumphant eyebrow, looking smug.

"Thought so," she replies, sinking back into the bubbles with her eyes closed. "Anyway, it's not that I'm opposed to this kind of thing. I think there's a certain romance in it, for sure. But I think sometimes simplicity is key. I don't lead a complicated life or have anything special about me. And I think most people would say the same of themselves. They want to find that reflected in their fiction."

"But like you said before—some people want to escape. Be taken somewhere new."

She opens one eye to look at me. "Not me," she says gently. My heart is beating so hard against my ribs that I'm surprised it's not sending ripples through the water. What is she telling me? That I'm too much for her? That she's unimpressed by me and my lifestyle? Surely after the fuss she kicked up, she can't be telling me that she's not interested?

We watch the rest of the sunset in silence. I keep an eye on the baby monitor, but Rosie is keeping quiet for the time being, at least. Part of me is hoping she'll rescue me from this scenario, but every other part of me just wants to stay here all night with India, talking about nothing. It always feels a little like this with her, I guess. Is that normal—to be so scared of a person, but so drawn to them at the same time?

Before I know what's happening, we're blanketed in darkness and India is getting out of the tub. I frown.

"Where are you going?"

India smiles, holding her hands out in front of her and examining them. "I was starting to wrinkle," she says. "And it's a work night, remember? It's going to be a long day tomorrow. Lots of conference calls lined up…"

"That's what you're thinking about right now?"

She shrugs. "Is there something else I should be thinking about?"

Work is the last thing on my mind when she's wearing a swimsuit like that, but I don't say that aloud. I just shake my head. I might be imagining it, but she seems a little disappointed. She grabs one of the towels that I brought outside and wraps it around her body.

"This was sweet," she says, tossing her damp curls over her shoulder. "But I don't need romance to be impressed. I just need to know that you're interested. I'm not as high maintenance as you might think."

I frown. "I don't think that."

India flashes me a knowing smile. "If you knew that, we'd be sitting inside right now, eating takeout. But in this case I'm glad you didn't know. Because the sunset was beautiful."

She heads back inside, her feet leaving behind soggy footprints on the patio. I sit back in the tub, wondering whether this evening was a success or not. She didn't start any arguments or get angry at me, but on the other hand she didn't seem particularly impressed by what I'd planned. After all of that I still don't know where I stand with her.

She said she just wants to know I'm interested. Have I not conveyed that already? Or do I need to do something else? Something bigger?

Perhaps I just need to take it back to basics.

Seventeen

India

Heading back into the house after the hot tub session, I wonder how the evening went. It's hard to tell whether I made a good impression or not. William always seems so edgy around me. Is it because he's hoping to impress me, or because I scare him?

I try to recall the conversation we had while we were outside. It all seemed to pass in such a blur, but all I can think is that I must have sounded so ungrateful. He put some thought into what we did for the evening, and all I did was put him down for it. Did I just mess up what was meant to be our final chance?

I know I'm overthinking things. William may be

shy in many ways, but he's passionate. If he dis-
agreed with anything I was saying, he would have
let me know. But I can't help thinking that I'm not
cut out to be with a guy like William. We're just so
different in every single way. He's wealthy; I'm not.
He's good-looking; I'm average. He's logical and I'm
creative. I know they say that opposites attract, but
is it possible to be too different? Is there any chance
that this can move forward, or are we too different?

While I dry off in the guest bedroom, I hear Rosie
crying and the soft chime of the doorbell.

I quickly finish changing back into my clothes and
hurry out to see if William needs my help.

He's already at the door, with Rosie in one arm
as he swings it open.

"Myrna, what are you doing here?" He sounds
surprised.

"I've been texting you all day," a female voice
says from beyond the threshold.

"I'm…" He clears his throat, glancing down at
Rosie. "I was busy, as you can see."

Frowning and feeling a little prick of jealousy, I
peer past his shoulder and spot a model-gorgeous
blonde with big blue eyes and a pouty red mouth.

She's the kind of woman who would never put
him down for treating her like royalty. The kind of
woman who would never call him spoiled or think
his lifestyle is too much for her, because she would
relish it in ways I can't even begin to know how to.

"I can't find my mother's earrings. I must have

left them here." She laughs softly and then peers past his shoulder, into his home, and adds, "Won't you let me look?"

"They're not here," William states.

"Please."

After a moment, William grudgingly steps aside. I notice the diamond earrings glinting in her ears and can hardly believe she has another pair.

"We broke up a while ago. You can't expect me to believe you're looking for earrings after all this time," William grumbles at her, a frown on his handsome face. He looks so adorable I wish I could just kiss the frown off his brow.

"Well, as I said, I can't find them and I've been looking everywhere. Oh…!" She pauses as she spots me and gives me an intense once-over while William shoots me an apologetic smile. "And she is?" the woman demands.

"My assistant." Will switches Rosie from one arm to the other, still looking at me with a silent apology in his eyes.

I nod at his ex with a shaky smile, feeling almost a little sorry for William. Because I can tell she's about as cold and mean as he is, or used to be, and yet in a sad way she also looks like everything I'll never be. I motion shakily to William. "I can take Rosie, so you guys can talk if you want."

"It's not really necessary—" William is still frowning, while Rosie is happily slapping at his jaw, oblivious to what's going on.

"Yes, thank you," Myrna says.

"Actually, if you don't mind, India."

Rosie giggles up at William, amused when she slaps his jaw again, the sound a little wet because she'd just been chewing on her fist.

I quickly approach to take Rosie from William's arms and get a whiff of his scent. Did he spray on cologne after the hot tub? I shiver when our fingers connect, our eyes meeting for a fraction of a second—a fraction of a second when my heart almost wants to leap out of my chest. My fingers itch from wanting to dry his jaw from Rosie's love slaps, but instead I quickly turn away with Rosie, blushing and trying to hide it as I carry her to her bedroom. Rosie is now slapping at me, and I'm catching her chubby hand before contact and making faces at her to make her giggle.

"Don't be a meanie, princess," I lovingly chide as we get to her room.

She giggles again.

And still…the voices from the living room carry over.

I should probably shut the door.

But I don't.

Why don't I?

Because I feel protective of William. Possessive. Because I'm so jealous, my stomach is cramped.

"I'm *wearing* my mother's earrings, William," Myrna is telling him with a soft laugh. "God, I can't believe you don't remember. I'm here because I'm willing to give you another chance."

A dead silence.

Then I hear William's voice, rough and deep and stony. "I'm not asking for one."

"Oh, come on. I know it hurt you when I broke up with you. But you're always so cold and selfish. But I've been thinking that… I miss you. I haven't been able to stop dreaming of you these past weeks. I just sense there's more to you, and right now when I see you, there's definitely something different."

"It's because you're no longer in my life, Myrna. I'd like to keep it that way."

"So there's someone else?"

"No." The emphatic way William says it almost makes me weep inside.

"But you want there to be? Oh, my gosh! How come I didn't see this sooner? Is it *her*? Your assistant?"

I gasp and raise my hand to stifle the sound.

"I really should get back to my niece," William says. "See yourself out, please."

"William, wait…"

A silence. There's no sound of footsteps, or anything at all except my own crazy heartbeat.

"We make sense. I'm a businesswoman—you're a businessman. Imagine the way we could combine our empires…"

"I don't need more work in my life," William answers firmly. "And I already have more money than I know what to do with."

"What do you need then?" she sounds frustrated, like this isn't playing out the way she wanted it to.

"Something normal, natural." William doesn't even hesitate when he answers. As if he already knows exactly what it is that he wants.

"Something that fills up the void? Nothing will ever fill it, William, not for men like you."

There's another silence. I hear the rustle of clothes and my stomach constricts as I imagine them kissing. I'm tempted to go out in the hall and peer toward the living room, and when I take a few steps in that direction, it's to see William halt her hand as she reaches for him and turn his face away when she tries to kiss him.

His ex sighs as he places her hand back at her side. "I'm not interested, Myrna," he says, softly but firmly.

She looks up at him, as if seeing him for the first time. "Wow. That was… I can't believe…" She shakes her head as if to clear it, taking a step back. "At least it's nice seeing you with your niece. It shows you actually have a paternal side."

"Do me a favor," William says as he walks her to the door. "Don't ever come looking for me at my home, or anywhere else for that matter, again. You were right when we broke up. There was nothing there. It's over."

By the time the door shuts, I'm trying to make

myself busy with Rosie once more. She's fussy and I know it's because she needs to eat, so I heat up the bottle and pretend I didn't hear a word they were saying as William walks into his bedroom.

"Hey," he says from the door. "Sorry about that. I have no idea what that was about."

"You don't?" I laugh. "I do. She wants you back, and I don't blame her."

Oops, did I say that out loud? I can't meet his gaze, for some reason. Is it true that he wants me? Could his ex tell?

"How did it go?" I ask, trying to cover for myself.

He's watching me quietly, his eyes twinkling as if he's just realized I may have heard. "What is it about women? Do they have some sort of radar to let them know that you've completely forgotten about them? Can they sense when you're so over them that they can't help but come back and try to wrap you around their fingers again?" He's teasing a little, but his eyes are intense, his brows raised as he watches me finish feeding Rosie.

"I don't know. I've never had that special connection with someone to sense…sense what's up with them."

But I feel connected to him…and hate not knowing if he feels the same way. Hate wanting something I cannot have.

I'm not a socialite. I'm not like Myrna. I'm…simpler. And maybe simple isn't the best thing for a man like William Walker.

Let's face it, William rejected me, the same way he just rejected her. It's not like he's really wanting more with me than possibly a friendship.

Once Rosie is fast asleep, I set her down on the crib, keenly aware of William standing by the window, his hands in his pockets as he watches me head to the door.

I pause there; his scent fills my nostrils for some reason. "Well, good night."

I wait for a heartbeat. Two. Waiting for something…for him to *say* something. But when he just looks at me, his jaw clenched as if he has no idea what to say, I quickly force myself to leave.

God. I'm so stupid!

I head to the office to gather my things, wishing that William was a little bit more forward and had asked me to stay. I know I told him that we couldn't touch tonight, but he's not exactly a natural-born flirt either. Still, part of me likes that he holds his cards closely to his chest. He's not like other men, who lay it on thick until they get what they want. William takes more careful, calculated steps. He might not be charging in, guns blazing, but I suspect when he finally gives me something to work with, it'll be totally worth the wait.

Somewhere in this huge house, William is processing the evening we shared too. I wonder if he feels the way I do right now—frustrated, curious, longing.

When did all of this become so complicated? It

was never this confusing with any of the guys I have dated. But then again I was never as exhilarated by them as I am by William. Though I still can't put my finger on why I'm so attracted to him, the fact is that he's the only man for years to get my heart beating a little faster. Not always for the right reasons, but he does regardless.

Just as I'm getting ready to call a car, there's a knock on the office door.

He doesn't wait for me to respond before opening the door. He looks a little hesitant for a fleeting moment but his eyes are full of energy. Passion. He steps into the room, shuts the door.

"Don't go."

"What are you—"

Then he kisses me, and all of tonight's carefully planned rules are out the window.

It all happens in a flash, and by the time I come back to my senses, we're in the guest bedroom. He's down to only a pair of tight boxers, and I've stripped to my bra and panties. Anxious for him. To feel his skin beneath my fingers. More of his kisses. More of this. I ease down onto the bed and beckon him over. He clicks off the light, our fast breaths echoing in the silent bedroom.

Then he's crawling onto the bed…above me. All of a sudden he's on top of me, his face hovering above mine. He sets the baby monitor on the nightstand with a soft thump, his gaze holding mine in the dark. I'm shaking with anticipation. As he trails one of his fingers down the side of my face, I hold my breath.

"Do you want this?" he asks. His fingers brush over my skin as he takes off my bra, grazing the skin at my throat. I shudder under his touch.

"Of course I do. This is what I've been waiting for."

His face dips between my breasts, his hot breath tickling my skin. His tongue trails upward, making me gasp as it touches my neck. His teeth graze my ear.

My underwear is soaked. I'm so turned on, so shocked by the turn of events, that I can barely process this.

Finally his lips lock on to mine. His tongue thrusts in, hot and candid, sipping me up like his favorite drink. I kiss him hungrily, my hands grappling for any part of him I can reach. It's messy and heated in a way I have never experienced before. Any sexual encounter I've had before has been slow and calculated. This is raw, hot, heavy. I can barely breathe, but I don't really mind. William is hard as a rock as he grinds against me.

"I've waited so long for this," he growls in my ear as our lips break apart for a moment. Goose bumps cover my skin.

"Tell me," I plead. William trails a hand down my body, slipping his hand into my panties. He finds me completely ready for him. He slides two fingers inside me and I sigh, leaning into his touch.

"I used to watch you at the office," he murmurs, kissing my breasts as he works up a rhythm. "And I'd think about how it would feel to touch you this way. To hold you against me. To have you."

I moan. This is exactly what I wanted to hear. I grind against his hand to make him go faster.

"I thought about you too," I tell him. I sit up to kiss his neck, gently pressuring my teeth against his skin. "When I was angriest at you, I'd imagine the make-up sex we'd have. How fiery it would be. How…rough you'd be."

He takes the hint and thrusts his fingers into me faster, his free hand grabbing my face and pushing my head back deeper into the pillow. It's so unlike him to do something like this that somehow it makes it sexier. He starts to use his thumb to strum my clitoris and I squirm in bliss.

"William…"

He moves to kiss my lips, his gentle side returning for a moment, though he's not tentative anymore. I can tell he wants this as much as I do. His tongue thrusts against mine, pushing and twisting.

I gasp as he works toward my first climax, my legs trembling as I reach the ultimate pleasure. My vision blurs and my hips buck toward him. I can't help crying out quietly, but William doesn't seem to mind. He slows his fingers down a little and then takes them out completely. I watch as he sucks his fingers dry, and he looks so good doing it that I practically hit the same high all over again. But now I want it to be my turn. I want to show him what I can do.

William is still in a commanding mood. He caresses my breast hard, teasing one of my nipples and pinching it.

I can tell he wants more of me. I can tell he wants *all* of me.

"I want you naked on top of me," he tells me. I don't have any desire to refuse him at all. I slip out from under the duvet and stand up, almost naked save for my panties. I look over my shoulder to check that he is watching. Of course he is. I don't turn around—not yet. He can wait a moment.

As I slip off my panties, I bend low, letting him get a good view of my ass. When I finally turn around, William's eyes are full of lust, one hand slowly stroking his cock as he drinks me in. I take my time clambering back onto the bed. The duvet is on the floor now—there's nothing to hide beneath. We're both completely exposed, and I can't think of anything sexier.

I'm on my knees on the bed, my hands stroking his muscular thighs. I can tell William wants me to touch him, but I think it's best to tease him a little first. He watches as my hand dips between my legs, my other hand exploring my breasts. His breathing grows heavier and he begins to stroke himself faster too, but I shake my head at him. He stops, but I can tell how difficult it is for him. He's so frustrated, fully erect, and I'm not doing anything about it. Still, his eyes wander over my body and I know he's feasting on me. Only when his eyes drift from my torso to my eyes do I move toward him.

I lower my mouth to his cock and begin to suck gently. William watches me intently, his eyes half closed as he relaxes. At first I use my hands, too, but each time I take him in my mouth, I let him in a little deeper. Soon I have his full length in my mouth and I'm moving faster now.

I admit that I fantasized about this, doing this under his desk, in the elevator, anywhere. But nothing can compare to the way he feels in real life, so thick and pulsing in my mouth, the way his scent makes me dizzy with want. He lets out a soft growl as I reach the head and lick and twirl my tongue around him.

William gasps, grabbing my hair as I suck him off. He's big enough to make the experience a little uncomfortable, but I don't care. I want to please him no matter what.

When he gasps a second time, I can tell it's time to step it up a notch. He's getting closer. He looks disappointed when I sit up at first, but when I straddle him, his eyes light up.

"That's right, that's what I want," he says gruffly with a lick to my neck.

God, he's so hard, so strong, as he leads me down onto him.

I'm no longer in control—not really.

He is. He sheaths himself with a condom and grabs my waist to guide me into position.

I'm a little nervous—it's been a while since I rode a guy. But as I allow him to slip inside me, filling me up, I forget to be nervous. I forget about everything.

The first few moments, I can barely move, I'm so turned on. William is content with that, letting me adjust to his size, his eyes drinking in every part of me—my hair, wild and free, the way my breasts rise and fall with each breath. My tiny waist, as he holds me down on him.

Suddenly I can't take it. I need more. More of him. All of him. I lean forward, licking his lips. Purring when he opens his mouth and gives my lips an even deeper lick.

I slowly begin to ride him, gasping each time his cock shifts inside me. I've never experienced something so intense with a guy. William seems to be experiencing something similar; his pupils are fully dilated and his jaw is clenched in pleasure. His muscles flex as he thrusts up and helps me move, his fingers digging into my skin as he sets the pace. I'm making so much noise that it's a good thing that William doesn't have neighbors anywhere nearby.

"I like hearing you moan," William groans against my neck, licking and kissing me, then biting down on his lip as he looks up at me, his gaze half-mast and reverent.

His words unleash me completely, and I don't hold

back. I allow myself to give in to my animalistic im-
pulses. I forget to be self-conscious. I ride him until
suddenly I'm crashing over the edge of my second
orgasm.

William groans deeply in his throat and I know
he's about to come. I allow myself to be taken over
by the pleasure, relishing the moment when William
spills inside me. I'm sweating and breathing hard,
but I don't care. We watch each other for a moment
before William grabs my hips and pulls me off him.
Then, to my surprise, he wraps his arms around me
and pulls me closely, kissing my face and my hair. I
sigh into him, feeling happier than I have in a very
long time. I can feel myself drifting toward sleep,
but my final thoughts before I give in are of William Walker.

Sleep doesn't last long.

I wake sometime later to the feel of lips wan-
dering along the back of my neck. I instantly know
who's cupping my breasts. Whose erection is pressing into my butt. Whose warm breath is caressing
my ear. My heart skips in excitement; I'm instantly
wide-awake and start to move in his arms until I'm
on my side, facing him.

His eyes gleam in the dark, and I think I can make
out a smile on his lips. I reach up to touch those lips,
stroking my fingers along them. He nips my finger-
tips playfully.

I groan and lean forward to playfully nip at his

jaw in reply. He chuckles softly and rolls me onto my back, and suddenly his soft chuckle is rumbling against my lips and spilling into me. His warm hands coast up my sides. He seizes one of my legs by the knee, folding it upward until he drapes it over his shoulder.

I gasp in shock, feeling completely opened up by William. He doesn't give me time to wonder what it's going to feel like to have him enter me like this. He simply drags his erection along my folds, up and down, up and down, those gleaming eyes watching me in the shadows as I grow more breathless by the second. And when I'm actually panting out loud, when I can smell how wet I am and how swollen my entrance feels, he retreats only to slide on a condom and start pushing in.

I have no words—the pleasure is too intense. The position allows him to go all the way in—every inch of me is filled to the hilt. I claw at his arms, rearing upward to offer him my mouth to take, as well. He takes it. Oh, he takes it, without a second's hesitation. William devours my every breath, tasting me as completely as he's physically taking me. My body tells him without words how much I want him. No man, in my whole life, has ever wanted me, cherished me or taken me quite like *this*.

The next time I wake up, it's to the silky touch of something wet and warm against me. I groan because it feels so good. Then I glance down and spot his dark head moving between my parted legs.

"Oh, God, William." I grab his hair, not knowing whether I mean to pull him closer to me or push him away because I'm in such a vulnerable, open position.

He turns his head and kisses the inside of my thigh, lifting his gaze to me. "Lay back. Let me taste you. You taste incredible. I've wanted to do this for a long, long time, India…" His breath bathes my folds before he tastes me again, and I feel myself sink into a liquid pool of lava as he continues feasting on me in a way that makes me feel sexier, more wanted—and has me coming harder—than ever before.

Eighteen

William

The moment I wake up is bittersweet, to say the least. On one hand I'm wrapped up in bed with a beautiful woman. On the other there's a baby monitor right next to me, and my niece is screaming bloody murder from the speaker.

India shifts in her sleep, stretching her arms. She rolls over to plant a peck on my lips. It's a far cry from last night, when we went at each other until the early hours of the morning. Multiple times, in every which way I could think of. I just couldn't get enough.

Now, with this tender morning kiss, it feels like

we've skipped five years down the line, like we're married with kids. It's a shocking thought, but it also makes me smile.

I feel sated, content and more relaxed than I've felt in a long time.

"If you go and make me a cup of coffee, I'll get Rosie fed and sorted out," she murmurs sleepily. I rub circles on her back. Her skin is incredibly soft and I can't get enough. I like the taste of it too. So much I could kiss her, head to toe, if only for the pleasure of tasting her. If Rosie wasn't crying, I'd be tempted to skip work and stay here all day, indulging in her.

"You don't need to do that," I assure her.

"I don't mind," she says with a sleepy smile. God, she looks good in the morning. She slips out of bed, completely naked, and starts dressing in her work clothes. It's a shame to see her fully dressed now that I've seen what's underneath, but I have to remind myself that she's still my assistant. I can't exactly ask her to work in her underwear.

Though a guy can dream.

She heads for the door but first, as if it's an afterthought, she returns to kiss my cheek.

She seems almost nervous as she does, as though she's not certain she should. I know the feeling—after a one-night stand with someone you know well, how do you act? Do you pretend like it didn't happen? Do you go for a kiss, hoping that the night was the beginning of something more? India opted for middle ground, and I lie in bed for a moment, wondering what that means. Is she waiting to see which way this will swing, or is she trying to decide how she wants this to go?

I slip out of bed, shower as quickly as I can and get dressed. Then I head to the kitchen in a daze to make India a coffee. I'm suddenly consumed by confusing thoughts that I'm not ready to confront. What do I want from India? What does she want from me? Are we better pretending that last night was just a fling, or do we acknowledge it like adults?

How has this become so confusing? There were no blurred lines last night when we were wrapped up in each other's arms. We knew we wanted each other, and without speaking, we could tell what the other wanted. She knew exactly how to use her mouth. She moaned to let me know I was doing exactly the right thing with my hands. But this morning, how can we communicate how we feel?

As the coffee machine brews two cappuccinos, I lean against the kitchen counter and try to formulate a plan. I want to let her know that, for me, last night wasn't a fluke. It wasn't a one-night thing that I'm happy to forget. I want this. I want her.

Maybe it'll freak her out, though. We've gone from enemies to lovers in less than a month. Would she be opposed to a relationship, especially so soon? Would she worry about what her family and friends think? I'll bet she's told them things about me that put me in a bad light. Not that I blame her, but it wouldn't help my case if I really want things to progress.

There's too much to think about. Maybe the key is not to think at all. Maybe I just need to take a chance for once and tell her what's on my mind. What's the worst that could happen? At the end of the week, we go our separate ways and don't speak again. If I never tell her how I feel, then that will happen anyway. But if I do, I might get the chance to keep her for a while longer.

With two coffees in hand, I slowly head upstairs. I psyche myself up, rehearsing lines in my head of what I can say to her. I can feel anxiety rising in my chest, my lungs constricted, my chest heaving as I fight for air. It's been a long time since I opened up to anyone, let alone a woman. I take a deep breath. It's going to be fine. What will be will be.

When I enter my bedroom, India has just finished changing Rosie. She tickles Rosie's belly and she giggles, kicking her chubby legs in the air. Then India looks up and smiles. It takes my breath away for a moment. I feel a rush of love out of nowhere, for both Rosie and India. And suddenly all of the words I wanted to say are reduced to nothing. How can I now possibly describe to her what I'm going through?

India puts Rosie back in her crib and then takes a coffee from my hands. I watch as she takes a long sip, her eyes closed. She looks at peace. It's a nice feeling to be the reason for that. I really want to say something to her, but my lips stay sealed.

India glances up at me, studying my face for a moment. Her forehead creases a little in confusion.

"Everything okay?" she asks. This is my opportunity; I should really say something. But when I open my mouth, nothing comes out. It's starting to seem odd. India is waiting expectantly, and I'm just standing here, gaping like an idiot. In the end I sigh. Smile. Shake my head.

"Everything's fine," I tell her.

The week passes blissfully. On Tuesday evening India heads home, giving me a friendly wave as she leaves the house. I spend the evening alone with Rosie, who screams all through the night. It doesn't bother me so much, though, because with thoughts of India rushing through my mind, I doubt I'd be able to sleep anyway. Each day, when she returns to work, I expect something to happen. I spend hours preparing lengthy, romantic speeches, only to allow them to fizzle on my lips each time I get close to saying something. We sneak glances at each other and secretive smiles, as though we're in a room full of people who don't know about the night we spent together. But we never mention it. We never get close to kissing, or even touching one another. We keep a professional distance, and my hopes of ever revealing my feelings to her seem to die. I try to accept that it was just one special night, but every part of me wants more. Now that I've had a taste of her, I crave her.

And yet she gives me no signs of how she's feeling. She smiles sweetly and makes me cups of coffee and makes general chitchat, but she never makes a move. Never pushes the boundaries. I begin to wonder if I did something wrong. Maybe she didn't enjoy the night as much as I thought. As Thursday comes and goes, I finally come to the conclusion that India is too good for me, and that she will forever be unobtainable.

It's Friday morning now. I didn't sleep much last night at all. Though Rosie slept peacefully through the night, I spent it tossing and turning, thinking about India. I suppose she could continue being my assistant. We've been working so well together now.

And I could buy myself sometime to warm her up to the idea of giving us a go.

But at the same time…will she feel used and diminished if I ask her to remain as my assistant after what happened—when what I really want is so much more?

Today is her final day in my employ. It's also my last chance, I suppose. If I'm going to say something, it has to be today or not at all. The thought fills me with anxiety. Maybe if things were more definite, I wouldn't feel this way, but I have no idea how things will go if I open up to her. All I know is I can let her go so easily.

She'll be here in an hour. Rosie snuffles and begins to cry softly, so I scoop her up and rock her gently, the way that India taught me to. Another thing to love about India—she taught me to connect with my niece. I kiss Rosie's forehead fondly, resting my tired eyes for a moment as Rosie begins to settle back down.

The quiet moment is broken by a FaceTime call. It's Kit. He hasn't FaceTimed me since last week, though he's texted me plenty of questions throughout the time he's been away. I rest Rosie on my lap to answer the call. Kit pops up on my screen, looking tanned and beaming with happiness.

"Yo, brother! You're an early riser today," he says, his voice filled with energy. I smile wearily.

"For once Rosie isn't the culprit for my sleeplessness. It's of my own doing, I guess."

"Well, you'll be pleased to know that it's only a few days until we come back and take the little rascal off your hands. Let us see her!"

I turn the camera so that Kit can coo at Rosie. Alex suddenly appears behind him.

"Hey, Will! *Ohhhh*, Rosie, how is my precious girl?"

Both Kit and Alex jabber on to her for five minutes straight, as though she knows what they're talking about, giving her details about their trip away and how much they miss her. When Kit finally tells me to turn the camera back around and Alex says goodbye, Rosie is completely out of it.

"We miss her little angel face," Kit says, drooping a little. "Has she been good? Is she doing okay?"

"Of course she is. She's struggling a little with the

teething, but she's good. I promise I've taken excellent care of her."

"I know, I know. It's just been hard leaving her for this long." Kit sighs, raking his hand through his hair. "We've had a good time, but we're ready to come back now. It's not the same being without her."

I smile. "You've gone soft, bro."

Kit grins at me. "Yeah, well, babies tend to have that effect." He shifts a little, and the image on the phone wobbles. "Anyway. How are you doing? Managing to fit in work okay?"

"Yeah, it's fine," I say absentmindedly. I've still got India in the back of my head. Kit gives me a knowing look.

"Someone's distracted."

"Hmm? No, I'm listening."

"You've got that assistant of yours on your mind. I can tell."

I roll my eyes. "Now, why on earth would you think that?"

"Because you have a massive love bite on your chest."

I glance down in panic. I'd forgotten about that. Kit laughs loudly, shaking his head at me.

"Oh, Will, you're so fucking unsubtle. Did you think I wouldn't notice that something was different?"

"Wait, how did you know it was India?"

"Oh, please, it's so obvious. From the very first day you hired her, you've been out of sorts and even more of a grump than you always are. It was clear you wanted her, bad. Plus Dad rang. He told me everything he knows."

I roll my eyes again. Trust Dad to tell all my secrets.

"So, come on. Spill the beans. What's going on with you guys? Are you sleeping together? Is she good in bed?"

"Don't be crude," I hear Alex saying in the background. Kit mumbles an apology, though he's waggling his eyebrows at me.

"Come on, bro, I want details."

"Well…" I smile.

"Damn. That good?" Kit raises an eyebrow. "Wow. You really like her, huh?"

I nod. This is going into very revealing territory. But Kit isn't teasing me anymore. He chews his lip, looking concerned.

"And does she feel the same?"

"I don't know. It's impossible to tell. We've been carrying on as normal. I get the feeling she just wants to forget about it all."

"Well, how will you know if you never ask?"

I shrug. "I guess I won't."

Kit lets out a long, despairing sigh. "Will, listen to me. You're only going to get one chance. If you let her walk away without saying anything, you could lose her for good. Is that what you want?"

"I… I don't—"

Kit is getting more and more frustrated. "Why

do you do this to yourself, man? You just back away at the first sign of a complicated feeling. You need to learn to open up and be honest. You're probably giving her mixed signals. How is she supposed to know how to act when you're not giving her anything in return?"

I think about all of the moments we've shared this week. Little things, like our hands brushing as she hands me a cup of coffee. Those moments when we smile at one another without any particular reason. Or when we try to pass one another in the corridor and both veer the same way and laugh. Am I not giving her the signals then?

"I'm no good at this. I don't want to push the limits."

"But that's the whole point. You have to if you want to move forward. Otherwise you'll be in this limbo forever."

"Well, not forever. It's her last day here today. I might never see her again."

"Exactly! So if you don't do anything now, you'll spend the rest of your days wondering what could've happened if you'd just stepped up and made a move. Stop waiting for everything to fall into place, man. Do something about it."

I know he's right. Kit's kind of like my nagging conscience—he always tells me what I already know, but what I need to hear out loud. But it's not as simple as that. I don't have his courage. I don't have his charisma, his charm or any of his best qualities. The qualities that have landed him with a perfect wife and a perfect child. There's a good reason he has those things when I don't. But I can't change who I am.

"No one's asking you to change," Kit says, as if reading my thoughts. "Just for a single moment, you need to push your boundaries. That's all it takes. And the payoff will be massive—I promise you. You think I didn't feel inadequate for Alex? For Cupid's Arrow? At some point what we most want, what really makes us better, requires us to step into our fullest potential. Let it happen."

I hear a knock on the door downstairs. It's her. Kit seems to register what's happening and gives me a reassuring nod.

"Remember everything I've said, bro. This is your last chance. Don't waste it."

He hangs up the call. I take a deep breath, gently lifting Rosie and putting her back in her crib. I hurry downstairs to let India inside like an eager puppy.

When I open the door, she's standing there, waiting with a smile on her face. Of course I read way too far into this. Is she happy to see me, or was she thinking of something else? She looks me up and down with a warm gaze as she steps inside.

"Nice work attire today," she murmurs as she eyes my black slacks and simple black button dress shirt. She doesn't touch me as she heads for the stairs, but just the tone of her voice, sweet like honey, is enough to give me goose bumps, as though she's caressed my skin with her slim fingers. I'm on edge again, thinking about everything Kit said to me.

Today is my final chance.

"Did you find a new assistant?"

I blink, looking up from my laptop. India has her feet propped on the desk, her laptop nestled on her legs. She's watching me carefully. I get the feeling she's looking for a certain answer, but what does she want me to say? That I'll never hire another assistant because she was so wonderful?

"Yeah, I think we're almost there," I say truth-fully. Human resources has narrowed it down to two candidates and I have interviews lined up with them on Monday. The good thing is that they can both start right away.

"Oh," India says after a few moments. She de-flates a little and takes her feet off the table. "Well, that's good. I wouldn't want you to fall behind or anything."

She doesn't sound very sincere, but I just nod. There's not much to say; it is what it is. India chews her thumb, mimicking an action I so often catch my-self doing. She's on edge. Is there something she wants to say to me?

In the end she just returns to work and I try to do the same, but she's all that's on my mind, as usual. In some ways I'm desperate for this day to end so I can be released from the confusion and the uncer-tainty. In other ways I'd rather keep this up forever than lose her completely. *Say something. Just do it,* I tell myself. But of course, I don't listen.

Five o'clock comes quicker than I wanted it to. I tried to make each minute drag. I tried to fill it with India. With her laughter, her sarcastic jokes, her sultry gaze. But all too soon it's over, and she's packing her laptop up for the final time. The words are on the tip of my tongue. *Stay. Stay with me.*

I remain quiet.

India stands there for a few moments, gripping her laptop bag tightly. She looks around the office almost lovingly. "Well, I was just getting used to this," she says with a humorless laugh. It gives me a pain in my chest to hear such a sad sound. Is she as gutted to be going as I am that she's leaving?

Tell her, Walker!

But my feelings are too alien to me. Too strong to voice aloud without feeling as if I'm ripping myself completely open here.

"Well...you're welcome to come here anytime you want," I tell her. She smiles, but it doesn't reach her eyes. She needs me to say more. She needs me to give her something solid to work with. *I want you here,* I should say. She hangs her head, avoiding my eyes.

"Maybe I'll pop in some time," she says without much conviction. And then comes the moment I've been dreading. She holds her hand out for me to shake.

I've left it too late. This is it.

I take her hand in mine. It's so small and warm

in my palm. I want to raise it to my lips and kiss her hand. I want to pull her in and embrace her. But I don't. She holds on for a little longer than she should, and then she slips away from my grip, wincing as if I squeezed too tightly.

Or as if it hurt to let go.

I curl my fingers into fists at my sides. Burning for her, from the inside out.

"It's been a pleasure…working for you these past couple weeks," she tells me. Then, with a curt nod, she turns and leaves, and I can't bear to watch the moment when she walks out of my life.

Me, the big shot who built his company from the ground up. Self-made millionaire, workaholic who will do anything to get what he wants. Except when it truly counts, I suppose. Because I couldn't muster the damn courage to tell India that I want her. *All* of her. Like I've never wanted *anything* in my life.

Damn it. Big shot? I've never felt like such a loser in my whole life.

I guess I've never really had anything I really cared about to lose before.

I sit for a long time in my room with Rosie. She's barely stirred all day, lying quietly in her crib without any fuss. I almost wish she'd wake up or cry to give me a distraction. I feel like there's a hole in my chest. A hole left by the beautiful assistant who just walked out on me.

Kit was right. I regret everything I didn't say.

My phone buzzes at my side. I sigh. I don't want to check the messages. They won't be anyone I want to hear from. But when my phone rings and I see my father's name on the screen, I give in. I know he won't stop until I answer. I pick up the phone irritably.

"What?" I snap.

"Watch your tone, son!" Dad says jokingly. "I hope you haven't forgotten about your date tonight. I'm sending the car to pick her up at half past six."

Date? "What are you talking about?"

"Don't you remember? India and I discussed setting you up on a blind date with her friend. Well, it worked out perfectly—India's roommate, Montana, has agreed to go. You have a reservation at Alinea at seven."

"Dad…"

"You can't cancel on the day—it's rude. You'll have to just suck it up."

"I don't want to go on a date with anyone. Especially not India's friend."

Dad sighs. "Look, son, I can tell something went on with India, and I'm sorry for that. But you need to be at that restaurant tonight. I'll be very disappointed if you don't show up. I'm sure you'll have a good time once you're there."

He couldn't be more wrong, but I'm too beaten down from the day to argue. I sigh, running a hand through my hair.

"Okay."

"I'll be there at half past six to look after Rosie. Wear a nice suit."

He hangs up on that note. I check my watch. I've got only forty minutes to prepare—I've been moping for over an hour. I sigh, forcing myself to stand up.

I guess life has to go on without India here.

Except now Rosie is having a temper tantrum. I rush to her and when nothing placates her, I decide she misses India. I hold Rosie in one arm and wave one of her favorite toys with the other. She blinks and grabs at it, then wails and throws it to the ground.

I groan as I carefully hold her to my chest while picking the toy back up. "You could be happy if you decided to play with this. Why so hard to please, Rosie?" I ask as I shake the colorful toy in front of her.

Rosie sniffles and blinks up at me.

I notice how miserable she looks and wonder if she knows—can feel—that I'm just as miserable or more. What's the point of having it all if I won't allow myself a shred of happiness?

Just like Rosie rejected her toy, I tossed it all away.

Now I realize that all of the previous failed attempts I've made at relationships don't really matter. I wanted what others had, including the perfect family to complete my empire. But never once was my heart really in it. My motives were wrong. Everything was...wrong.

India is another story. I want things to work out with her so much that I can't think of anything else, nor will I be able to, until I've told her everything that needs to be said.

Realizing that, I calm down, and Rosie calms too, reminding me of how India once explained that trick to me. I set Rosie in the crib in my bedroom with her toy and start getting ready.

Once my dad arrives to take care of Rosie and I'm set to go, I grab my keys and head to my car. As I get in and check out the collar of my shirt and my clean shave in the rearview mirror, I know I'm dressed to impress. But it's definitely not to impress India's friend.

No. This is for *her*.

So instead of heading to the restaurant, I drive straight to India's apartment. This is the first time in my life I'm not thinking of what's right or what's expected of me or the consequences. This is the first time in my life I stand up a woman at a restaurant. Because I'm going after the one I want to be *mine*.

I find a parking spot across the street and pull to the curb. I step out of the car, shut the door and quickly cross the street to ring her buzzer.

I'm nervous about showing up unannounced, but at the same time I've never been so certain in my life of what I want. I'm not willing to spend another day without speaking my mind.

"Yes?" an unfamiliar female voice comes through the intercom.

"India?" I ask.

"She's out. Who is this?"

"William. William Walker."

"Her boss?" the woman on the other end screeches. Suddenly there's silence. I frown at the intercom, trying to figure out what to do for a minute. Then the front door jerks open and a woman in a silky nightgown opens the door.

"William Walker?"

"Who are you?" It's definitely not India.

"I'm India's roommate."

"Montana?" I gape. Wasn't she supposed to be meeting me? At the restaurant? What sort of joke is this? Montana seems to be puzzling over the same thing.

"You stood India up to come see her at her place... for any reason in particular?" She's eyeing me cautiously.

"I didn't intend to stand India up. I was standing up—"

"Me, of course," she drawls, a wry smile on her face. "Because it's not me you're interested in?"

I shake my head. "No."

She laughs and her gaze softens as she eyes me. "That's okay, I can take the broken heart. My roomie, however, puts up a brave front, but she has a soft heart under there. Don't squish it. And I hope you're not like the bad boss she told me about, but more like the man who's recently swept her off her feet without knowing it. Go on! She's at the restaurant."

I shake my head, stunned. "So you planned this?"

She nods, then shrugs. "Not me exactly. It was

your dad's idea. He wanted me to tell India to meet *him* for dinner at the restaurant to discuss what he was going to do with you. But then he was going to send you instead."

"Why?"

"He was convinced you needed a second chance with her but maybe she wouldn't go if she thought you'd be there. But I didn't trust you and only went along with his plan on one condition. You had to pass a test."

"A test?"

"Of your loyalty."

"What are you talking about?"

"You thought you were going on a date with me, but really the one we were planning to go all along was—"

"Her." I can barely say the word; my chest feels like it's just expanded a couple inches with love for my dad and India.

"Right. By coming here, you proved it's India who you want—and from the look on your face, you've got it bad. But if you'd gone to the restaurant first, thinking you were meeting me, I'd have proof you weren't right for her. You passed the test. Now go get her before it's too late."

"Thanks. Oh, nice meeting you." I dash back to my car but hit terrible traffic and ultimately arrive at the restaurant forty-eight minutes late.

A waiter shows me to my table and I immediately notice there's an unopened wine bottle, but no India.

"I'm sorry, sir," the waiter says. "She waited for about half an hour. She must have left."

A low growl of frustration leaves me as I plunge a hand through my hair and stalk out. Dammit. My only chance to take India out on a date and I blow it? I head out and dial her cell phone. No answer.

Hoping that if she went home, Montana would tell her I'm looking for her, I head home in search of my dad.

I open the door and walk in, and immediately I spot my father across the living room on the sofa, but he's too busy laughing with someone.

When the stunning female figure turns in my direction, I stop cold.

"India." I'm stunned. Blown away by how gorgeous she looks. And the fact that she's here. In my home.

"William."

She smiles at me as she comes to her feet. My damn pupils hurt; she looks so incredible. Her eyes are smoky and sultry, her lips coated in gloss. Her hair is wild and natural, and the dress she's wearing shows off her every curve. But it's her smile that I focus on. I thought I might never see it again.

"I've been calling you." My voice sounds rougher than I anticipated.

"Oh." She glances at her purse. "Sorry, I didn't hear it ring. Your father has been telling me how he and Montana set us up. After I waited at the restaurant for a while, I called him and he told me to come here. Where did you go?"

"I went to look for you. At your place. That's when Montana explained…"

"Oh!" she says, her eyes glimmering with realization. "You were looking for me there."

"That's right. Then I tried to catch up with you at the restaurant but got into traffic."

We both stare at each other in silence. I can barely believe she's here. No wonder Dad was so desperate for me to go on this date. He didn't set me up with Montana; it was India he wanted me to be with all along. But he and Montana sure made us work for it.

Damn, this woman is so perfect, I'm out of breath, out of words. I stand still, not quite knowing what to say or do. I want to take her hands and tell her how I feel, but I also want to rip her clothes off. It's not a good combination of feelings, but I can't help it. I'm so happy to see her.

Ignoring my father's cheerful, "Well, hello to you too, son," from somewhere in the living room, I ask her, "Have you had dinner?"

India shakes her head.

I cross the room to greet her, set my hands on her shoulders and rub her bare arms. She gazes back at me with warmth as I take a deep breath, trying to get my thoughts in order.

"I need to talk to you," I tell her, quietly. She raises her hand to grip my shoulder. Then she leans in and kisses me on the cheek. It doesn't matter that we're standing in front of my dad—it's like we're the only two people here.

I pull her closer by her waist, pressing her against me. Her hands fist on my shirt. I kiss her, flat out kiss her lips. Hard. When she pulls away, we're both a little breathless. We chuckle to ourselves, leaning our foreheads together.

"Does that sum up what you're thinking?" she asks.

I smile. "Pretty much perfectly. But there's more. Do you have some time?"

She nods.

It takes some effort for me to pull my gaze free of India's and glance at my father. "Dad, would you mind watching over Rosie for another couple of hours?"

"Hours? I was planning on spending the night." Dad motions to the small duffel bag at his side, grinning.

I smile in return, walking up to him to set a hand on his shoulder and give him a grateful squeeze. "How did you manage?"

"Well—" Dad's eyes glint as he glances past my shoulder, at India "—I had some help. This would have never worked if I didn't know who the young lady you were truly interested in was." He leans closer. "And it would have never worked if she hadn't stayed when I told her what the real plan was just now."

At my surprised look, he chuckles as he slaps my

back, lowering his voice. "She's a keeper, son, as are you. Now go, have some fun, you two. I'm looking forward to quality time—honing my Grandpa Daycare skills with Rosie tonight."

"Dad, are you sure you can—"

"Go! I raised two boys and you're both fine, aren't you?" He shoos me away.

With India waiting for me across the room, I can't resist the temptation to finally steal her away for the night.

Nineteen

India

"Do me the honor of having dinner with me, India Crowley?"

I nod at William's request, unable to believe that it's me to whom William extends his arm to escort out of the house.

Before leaving earlier today, I battled with telling him how I felt even as I sensed he was waging his own war. I battled with my own insecurities and doubts about being able to be the kind of woman that a man like William Walker, the rich, super-successful big shot, could ever love.

Now he's asked me to dinner—and I said yes, and there's nowhere else I'd rather be but with him.

"We lost our reservation," he tells me as he drives us to a surprise destination.

"That's okay. We can just get takeout—I'm simple. Like I've said before."

"Takeout? Okay." He drives us to the nearest fast-food restaurant and orders us two large cheeseburgers with fries and drinks at the drive-through. When we get our food, he takes us to Navy Pier.

He grabs the bags of food with one hand as I take the drinks. He helps me out of the passenger's seat with his free hand and never removes it from my arm as he leads me to a place to sit by the water.

I'm shaking from all of the things I want to say but can't seem to find the words for. I love him. It's exhilarating and frightening. I've never been in love before. I'm afraid to be in love with *him.*

William gazes out at the water, his food untouched. Honestly I haven't eaten mine either. I just study his profile, noticing the way he suddenly slips his hand in mine and squeezes it to get my attention. My skin tingles on contact.

"So. I suppose you might be wondering why—"

"You didn't go to dinner with Montana," I interrupt.

William smiles slowly as his gaze roams my features, a look of expectation in his eyes as an amused smile settles on his lips.

Tell him, India. Just let your guard down and tell him!

I open my mouth to speak, but nothing comes out, and instead I'm feeling my blush creep up my cheeks.

William seems amused by this. I suppose I always have some retort for him, but there he goes and leaves me speechless today.

He strokes the pad of his thumb down my jawline. "I'm not, nor have I ever been, interested in your friend, India. Or anyone else since you started working for me. Since day one… I've been obsessed, preoccupied, confused and taken with *you*."

I'm shell-shocked by his admission. A moment passes, then another. I inhale a shaky breath even as William laughs softly.

"The first day I saw you," he admits, watching me closely for a reaction, "I wanted you. Against my own wishes. Against every instinct that told me to run in the other direction. I ignored it as best as I could. I've tried to do what I felt was the right thing, even if it meant pushing you away more rudely than I intended to. But that only feels wrong now, India. Not being with you is wrong. Being scared of the best thing that's ever come into my life feels wrong—not to mention incredibly foolish." He grins.

I laugh disbelievingly. "You're scared of me?"

He thinks about it, frowning. "I admire you. I want you. I'm not scared of you. But I'm scared of the way you open me up. And the way I've fallen for you…completely."

He sounds so apologetic, almost as if he's not sure his love will be well-received. My throat feels thick with emotion.

"That's not enough to stop me anymore. I'm hard-working, India. I will work hard at this—"

"You don't need to," I interrupt. "William, yes, we had a rough start, but I played a part in that. I pushed every single button of yours I could. You scared me too. You still do."

He lifts my hand to set a kiss on my knuckles, a playful gleam in his eyes. "Don't be scared of me. You've seen the worst of me—I swear. There's another side to me you bring out, and I'd love you to meet this man, India."

"I already have." *He loves me! He loves me too!*

In some ways I knew. After he made love to me, this whole week—his stolen touches, his glances, every empty space between every spoken word. I knew. I *know him.*

In some intuitive way, I know him better than anyone.

I just can't resist setting a kiss on his lips and snuggling into his arms, breathing him in as I clutch the lapels of his collar. "Take me somewhere."

He strokes his hand along my back, whispering in my ear, "Where?"

"Anywhere we can be alone, in private."

He uses one fist to pull my head a few inches back and gives me a long, wet, delicious three-minute kiss that leaves my toes curling. We keep stealing kisses on the way to the five-star hotel on the bustling Miracle Mile, where he checks us in.

"I really don't need a fancy room. I would have been happy in the back seat of your car and—" He silences me with a finger to my lips as he shuts the door of the suite behind him.

"I'm not happy with half-assing this. Not this. Not with you. So let me. Okay?" He boosts me up in his arms as he carries me down a long hall, and I know he won't have me denying him this. William won't have it any other way. I actually hear myself giggle— I'm so happy—breathless as I wrap my arms around his neck.

He sets me down on the end of the enormous king-size bed, then unfastens the buttons on my dress and eases it off my shoulders. As he drags the fabric down my arms, he ducks to set a hot kiss on the top swell of my breast. He gives a little lick to my skin. Then he reaches up to my bra and pulls down the lace, exposing the pebbled peaks of my nipples.

He drinks in the large areolas and the hardened tips, and hungrily flicks out his tongue to lick the left one again in a deliberately slow circle before covering the peak with his mouth and sucking. I groan. William cups my breast and squeezes it between his palm and fingers as he turns his head to my other nipple. He gives it the same treatment, tasting me as if he's desperate to.

His hair is in my fists. I'm pulling him closer,

my world tilting on its axis as a wave of sizzling hot pleasure shoots through me.

I'm scared by how intense this is. I pull back and a harsh breath leaves me.

William jerks back in confusion. A lock of hair falls over his forehead. He looks gorgeous and I want him so much. He narrows his eyes, breathing low and harsh.

"You're scared? I am too, but I won't hurt you. I promise you. If I ever get out of line, *you* more than anyone, India, know exactly how to tame me." I bite my lower lip, smiling at the way he teases me, because he's right. I do know how to handle him, and yet all I want is the chance to love him.

Dragging in a ragged breath, I lean up and impulsively kiss his hot, hard lips. I again fill my hands with fistfuls of his hair and clench my fists even harder as he starts kissing me back. Kissing me like I'm all he wants.

He frames my face in his big hands, devouring what I'm offering, then slides one hand down my body—down, *down* between my breasts, along my abdomen, dipping it between my legs, then pulling my skirt up and sliding his hand back down to push my thighs apart and stroke me over my panties.

I gasp at the touch, welcoming it. Craving it.

He eases the fabric of my panties aside and drives one finger inside me. I arch up and rock my hips to his touch. "Yes." I groan.

He's watching me, his gaze hooded and his lashes heavy.

"I can't even find the words to describe how gorgeous you look right now," he rasps as he tugs my panties down my legs. He flings them over his shoulder, onto the floor behind us.

I'm fully naked now. I reach out to unbutton his crisp white shirt as quickly as I can even as he unzips his trousers and whips off his belt.

He removes his shirt and discards his trousers, along with his black boxers. He stands before me, fully naked, a dark-haired Adonis I want to binge on just like I know, sense, *feel*, that this Adonis wants to binge on me.

His erection stands tall and proud. His body is well-defined and athletic, his taut, tanned skin stretching across miles and miles of muscles. My eyes run over him, drinking in the dusting of hair along his chest, the admirable six-pack, once again to pause on his pulsing, thickened erection—and the way a drop of moisture shines at its tip.

I swallow eagerly.

William's lips curve sinuously as he notices my admiration. He leans over me, running a hand down my front, stopping to circle one of my nipples with his thumb, then the other, with expertise.

He drags that wicked thumb down over my belly button, to the V-shape between my legs, caressing me there.

"You're so sexy and so eager, India."

"Aside from the other night with you, I guess it's because it's been…a long time," I confess.

His expression gentles. His voice thickens. "I'm glad somehow that you haven't been with anyone for a while. At least…not with anyone while you've been working with me?" He waits for my answer.

I'm panting as his fingers trail down my stomach, down my hips and sides of my legs, then slowly up the inside of my thighs.

I shake my head, then nod, confused by his question. "Yes. No. I mean…there's been no one since I've worked for you. You've kind of made it hard for me to have a life after what you've put me through."

"Are you saying I need to make it up to you?" He sounds amused. My blood keeps boiling. He looks masculine, confident, sexy.

God, help me, he looks like a man *in love* with me.

As he lays me down and starts descending to kiss me, I pull him closer, my greedy hands on his buttocks, urging him to fill me. No more foreplay. No more pauses. No more excuses.

A low moan escapes me. The pleasure of our connection, the pleasure of feeling him—hard, hot, pulsing—his skin brushing against mine, is overwhelming.

"God, William." I groan.

"I like it when you say my name. Say it again and kiss me, my hungry, beautiful India."

I do as he asks.

He drives in at that moment, and the utterance of

his name ends in a groan. I clutch him tighter, and William feasts on my mouth, pulling out and repeating the thrusting motion, setting up a rhythm. He's got my wrists in his hands, both of them, pinned at my sides. My whole body arches up to his. I take every thrust and meet it with a roll of my hips. Every thrust pushes me closer to the edge, until I'm trembling from the pleasure. From the anticipation, the tension building inside me.

He feels amazing. He tastes amazing. He sounds so hot.

His burning blue eyes fix on me as I thrash beneath him, caught between wanting to savor every moment and an explosion that I'm afraid will tear me apart, one I will never recover from.

I should be scared. I *am* scared, but I'm too helpless to resist him, delirious with happiness and with desire. I lean up to meet him, kiss for kiss, touch for touch, my hips rocking in rhythm with his.

Every moment we've shared, every confession, has been like peeling off each other's clothes, allowing us to see each other as we really are. What I see delights me, excites me, challenges me, confuses me and obsesses me.

I can't get enough of him now.

He smothers my lips with his. "Do you understand now?" he rasps against my lips. He tears free and looks down into my eyes with a gaze that seems to carve into my soul. "Why I pushed you away…

India, do you understand me now? It was like I knew it would be this...this life-changing."

I find myself nodding, gasping, "Yes," and a brief smile tugs his lips before his mouth descends to mine again.

"Well, bring it now," he says and then groans against my mouth, lifting me up and holding me against his chest, kissing me senseless as he keeps driving inside me.

I shatter. I shatter into a million and one pieces, and then each of those pieces shatters into a million *more*.

His name leaves my lips in a reverent gasp as I shudder and shake in his arms. Dimly, I'm aware of William's tensing above me, against me, my name leaving his throat in a low, thick groan as he follows me there.

Moments after, he sets a kiss to the top of my head and brushes a damp tendril of hair behind my ear. "You're gorgeous, Miss Crowley."

There's a calmness in those sexy, heavy-lidded eyes as he looks down at me. He almost looks...at peace. If it wasn't for that gleam of hunger that still lurks in the very depths of his irises. A hunger that makes my own hunger claw its way back up.

Will I ever get enough of him?

I look into his eyes and find myself smiling in answer to his question, and as his own wicked smile appears in answer, I wonder, *Where have you been all my life? How could I have gone on another day without this?*

I'm so taken by him that I can't stop trailing my fingers up and down his body, watching his muscles constrict, as if he can't help reacting to my touch.

I giggle, and he frowns. "What's so funny?"

I raise my hand and stroke the stubble on his jaw with my fingers. "You." I run my eyes over his rumpled hair and his swollen lips. "You're cute."

"Cute?" He sits back, appalled and puzzled. "I'm pretty sure that's the last word anyone would use to describe me."

"Would you rather I try another?"

"Go right ahead." We both smile as I prop the pillow behind me and sit up in bed.

"Strong. Confident."

He keeps waiting for more.

I'm starting to laugh because I do find this man cute.

He lifts one brow. "Nothing about my prowess?"

"Ahh, *and* a fisherman too. Apparently he's already out fishing for compliments."

Smirking devilishly, he pulls me to him and rolls me on the bed until his body stretches above mine. "If you didn't immediately think of the word, then I must have done a bad job. Let me try again, sweet Miss Crowley."

I'm laughing softly when he descends, and my laugh fades into a soft sigh of pleasure as we start all over again.

* * *

We're back at Will's house the next morning. I got no sleep last night, but am eager to see Rosie before her parents pick her up.

"You sure it's okay for me to stop by and see Rosie before heading home?"

"I insist," William says, brushing his fingers along my bare back as he opens the door with his other hand.

We're greeted by intense bawling and William's dad looking about as panicked as he's ever looked.

"William! Thank God! She doesn't want to eat. I changed her diaper. I have no bloody clue," his father says as he tries passing Rosie to William.

William scoops her up. "Let's see if warming up her bottle will do it," I whisper to him as I hurry to the kitchen to warm it while William tries to rock her.

Rosie is calm and hiccupping from crying so hard by the time I return.

"You want to do it, or do you want me to?" I ask William as I show him the bottle.

"Here. You try it. Let me help my dad out. He looks ready for a long nap." William winks at me, and I smile at Mr. Walker and settle down on the couch, shifting Rosie's weight in my arms as I offer her the bottle.

I hear the men's voices as they talk in the foyer, and William's especially makes my stomach constrict with a warm feeling.

"...haven't had a night like last night in my life. Thank you, Dad."

"I'm glad. I don't know what you do for each other, but looks like it's more powerful than a vitamin shot laced with adrenaline."

I hear William laugh, and the door shuts shortly after, and then there's silence. I make sure Rosie is still sucking on the bottle and that it's angled properly so that she's not drinking air.

Confirming that everything is perfect, I look up to catch William with arms crossed, leaning back on his heels, looking at me like a real big shot from across an expanse of shiny marble floor.

I feel myself flush. "What?" I ask nervously, not used to being the focus of a man's intense appreciation like his.

"You look good with my niece in your arms."

"Just because I'm single doesn't mean I don't have natural motherly instincts," I retort, then glare at him. "But don't get any ideas."

He shakes his head. "I am. But they can wait. Come here." He sits down next to me and tucks me into his arm, embracing me and peering over my shoulder as I feed his niece. I suddenly feel like dozing off in his arms just like Rosie, and turn to rest my head against his chest.

"If I'm dreaming...don't ever wake me up, Walker," I beg, laughing softly when he just chuckles and sets a kiss on the top of my ear. He's the best uncle in the world. Best *man* in the world.

And me? The happiest girl on the planet.

Epilogue

India

"I can't help being nervous, Will. It feels like a big step."

It's Sunday morning. Well, it's midday, to be exact, and neither William nor I have made any move to get out of bed. This is the fourth consecutive weekend we've spent at my place, lying in late and watching TV together. We like the coziness of my place, and I love how down-to-earth—and close—William feels here. For two workaholics, we're getting much better at relaxing.

But today William wants me to officially meet his family—while he announces our engagement.

"Hey, relax," he says, stroking my hair gently. "It doesn't have to be a big deal. You've met my dad. And Rosie, of course. You used to speak with Kit all the time over the phone. That just leaves Alex, for now. No big deal."

"William, it took you two weeks to even come over here because you were scared of meeting Montana."

William laughs. "Yeah, well, you told me she didn't approve of me. And our first meeting wasn't exactly smooth."

"Come on, that night you came over looking for me, she changed her mind about you and *loved* you. Plus my family already loves you. So that gives me a lot to live up to. I don't want to mess this up."

He kisses my forehead gently. "As if you could. Look, you and Alex are going to get on like a house on fire. She's just as gutsy as you. And my family will be thrilled that you're my fiancée."

"I guess. But still, I have a right to be nervous. It makes this all very…official."

He pulls me in closer to his bare chest, letting me trace circles on it with my fingers.

"Well, I would say we're doing well, wouldn't you? Moving forward and all that?"

I nod quietly. I love him, and he feels the same too. We're moving forward. Setting a wedding date for next year. Becoming man and wife. Getting better at this whole thing of being a couple.

I even like Will's new assistant and helped her settle in. I work from my apartment during the week,

then meet him after work, helping him organize any
pending things at the office. Sometimes I write my
novel while I wait for him. And the rest of the time,
it's just him and me. Like this.

After four months of dating, it feels completely
natural to have taken this step. I'm elated, in love
and simply too eager for everything to be perfect
not to be nervous today when we drop the news to
his family.

"We can wait, if you're that nervous," William
says quietly. He's clearly reading my mood. But I
want to please him and, despite the nerves, can't
wait, so I shake my head with a smile.

"No, it's okay. Let's do this."

I start to get up, but he grabs my waist and pulls
me back into bed. I laugh as he straddles me, grinning
down at me like an excitable teenager. He kisses me.

"We can wait a little longer," he says, kissing his
way down my body. I let him take off my pants, and I
close my eyes, forgetting for a while the big day ahead.

We arrive at Kit's around 3:00 p.m. I'm dressed
casually, and seeing his house makes me feel like
I'm in rags. It's even bigger than William's and more
over the top. I shrink in my seat, but William senses
my nerves and grabs my hand.

"It's going to be okay," he tells me, and because
he's the one who said it, I believe him.

We head up to the house hand in hand. We're
barely at the door when Kit opens it, grinning like a

madman. I've met him several times before, but he's more handsome than I remember. He looks older, too, possibly as a side effect of becoming a dad. Before I can stop him, he throws his arms around me in a massive hug.

"India! I'm so glad we're finally doing this. Now I can actually speak to you in person instead of over the phone," he says. "I hope your wit is up to scratch in person too."

Now that he's put me on the spot, I feel the pressure to say something clever, but fortunately Kit has already moved on to greeting William. "All right, brother. Come on in. Rosie's missed you."

I step inside, sticking close to William's side. We head to a lounge area, where Alex and Alistair are enjoying a whiskey. Alex is beautiful—all vibrant red hair and catlike eyes—but I don't feel intimidated as she stands to shake my hand. She smiles sympathetically at me.

"Hey, India, nice to finally meet you. Thanks so much for helping William out with Rosie while I was away. I know she can be a handful."

"She was pretty sweet the whole time, but God, that girl has a pair of lungs," I say easily. Alistair laughs, standing to greet me too.

"I can already tell you're going to fit in with this lot," he says, patting my arm. "We're glad to have you here, India. You've put a smile on my boy's face. That's more than I ever hoped for."

William winks down at me as I smile up at him.

It's suddenly clear to me how much this meeting meant to him. He's opened up to me a lot over the past four months, saying how much pressure he's felt to find someone and settle down the way Kit did. I know now that my being here is the best gift I could give him. It's come hand in hand with his father's approval too. When Alistair smiles at his son, I can feel the tension between them melting away until all that's left is love and respect.

We spend a blissful day together. Alex and I share our dirtiest jokes. Kit and I play Ping-Pong until our wrists hurt. Alistair talks to me for half an hour about whiskey and I pretend to know what he's talking about. William and I tend to Rosie when she needs changing, giving Kit and Alex an opportunity to curl up on the sofa together and watch a film. And through it all, William's by my side. Touching my back each time I seem nervous. Filling my glass each time it gets empty. Laughing the loudest at my lamest jokes. Without a word shared between us, I feel love like I've never felt it before.

When it comes time to make our big announcement after dinner, I'm not nervous at all. When William stands up, draws me to my feet and tells his family that we're going to get married, I feel surrounded by their joy and love. I lean into William's chest, trying to remember a time when I felt this happy.

"You okay? You seem kind of deep in thought," he says after we've arrived home at his place later in the evening. I tilt my chin to look up at him, smiling.

"I'm just reflecting on today. I can't believe how happy I am. But I miss Rosie."

"You don't need to miss her for long."

"What? If you're implying I want to have a baby on the very day we announced our engagement—"

He laughs, pulling me closer. "I'm implying we can babysit anytime. But now that you mention it, I'm more interested in the act it takes to *make* a baby."

"Oh, are you?"

He nods somberly. "I'm…sort of addicted. To this act. To be honest."

We're both laughing as he pulls me into his arms. Then suddenly we're kissing—hard and fast, with joy and a need for connection.

I sink into the kiss.

I never believed that I could love kissing William the way I do. Love spending time with him. Being a part of his life. I never believed I would constantly battle with this craving to be a part of him…for him to be a part of me.

So when he gathers my dress up at the small of my back and tugs down my panties, I have nothing to say. I curl my arms around his neck and whisper "Yes" in his ear. Eagerly I curl my legs around his waist, and let him carry me to the nearest surface. He sets me against the wall, pulling open his fly, never once taking his mouth off mine. Not even as he braces me against the wall and holds me by the hips as he thrusts into me. Not as he starts moving, deeply and strongly, making me moan into his mouth even as he groans into mine. Not as he drags his mouth down my neck, then up again, to devour my gasps once more. Not a single moment do we stop kissing each other, and even when we're done it's like we can't get enough.

For two weeks we lived in our own little world, a pretend family—William, Rosie and me—and a part of me dreaded imagining what things would be like when Rosie's parents picked her up and I had to leave.

I was afraid because I didn't know what I was to William or what he was to me.

But now I know, and he knows.

And it is fun and fresh and new. It's like a date that never ends.

A date where we end up falling even more for each other every day.

* * * * *

If you liked William,
make sure you didn't miss
his brother Kit's story,
BOSS
by New York Times
and USA TODAY *bestselling author*
Katy Evans.

Available exclusively
from Harlequin Desire.

COMING NEXT MONTH FROM

✦HARLEQUIN® *Desire*

Available September 3, 2019

#2683 TEXAS-SIZED SCANDAL
Texas Cattleman's Club: Houston • by Katherine Garbera
Houston philanthropist Melinda Perry always played by the rules. Getting pregnant by a mob boss's son was certainly never in the playbook—until now. Can they contain the fallout...and maybe even turn their forbidden affair into forever?

#2684 STRANDED AND SEDUCED
Boone Brothers of Texas • by Charlene Sands
To keep her distance from ex-fling Risk Boone, April Adams pretends to be engaged. But when a storm strands them together and the rich rancher has an accident resulting in amnesia, he suddenly thinks he's the fiancé! Especially when passion overtakes them...

#2685 BLACK TIE BILLIONAIRE
Blackout Billionaires • by Naima Simone
CEO Gideon Knight demands that Shay Neal be his fake fiancée to avenge his family. Too bad he doesn't realize they already shared an anonymous night during the Chicago blackout! But even through the deception, the truth of their chemistry cannot be denied.

#2686 CALIFORNIA SECRETS
Two Brothers • by Jules Bennett
Ethan Michaels is on a mission to reclaim the resort his mother built. Then he's sidetracked by sexy Harper Williams—only to find out she's his enemy's daughter. All's fair in love and war...until Harper's next explosive secret shakes Ethan to his core.

#2687 A BET WITH BENEFITS
The Eden Empire • by Karen Booth
Entrepreneur Mindy Eden scoffs when her sisters bet she can't spend time with her real estate mogul ex without succumbing to temptation. But it soon becomes crystal clear that second chances are in the cards. Will Mindy risk her business for one more shot at pleasure?

#2688 POWER PLAY
The Serenghetti Brothers • by Anna DePalo
Hockey legend and sports industry tycoon Jordan Serenghetti needs his injury healed—and fast. Too bad he clashes with his physical therapist over a kiss they once shared—and Jordan forgot! As passions flare, will she be ready for more revelations from his player past?

**YOU CAN FIND MORE INFORMATION ON UPCOMING HARLEQUIN® TITLES,
FREE EXCERPTS AND MORE AT WWW.HARLEQUIN.COM.**

HDCNM0819

SPECIAL EXCERPT FROM

For Vanessa Logan, returning home was about healing, not exploring her attraction to cowboy Jacob Dalton! But walking away from their explosive chemistry is proving impossible…

Read on for a sneak preview of
Lone Wolf Cowboy *by* New York Times *and* USA TODAY *bestselling author Maisey Yates.*

She curled her hands into fists, grabbing hold of his T-shirt. And she had no idea what the hell was running through her head as she stood there looking up into those wildly blue eyes, the present moment mingling with memories of that night long ago.

While he witnessed the deepest, darkest thing she'd ever gone through. Something no one else even knew about.

He was the only one who knew.

The only one who knew what had started everything. Olivia didn't understand. Her parents didn't understand. And they had never wanted to understand.

But he knew. He knew and he had already seen what a disaster she was.

There was no facade to protect. No new enlightened sense of who she was. No narrative about her as a lost cause out there roaming the world.

He'd already seen her break apart. For real. Not the Vanessa that existed when she was hiding. Hiding her problems from her family. Hiding her feelings behind a high.

PHMYEXP0819

Hiding. And more hiding.

No. He had seen her at her lowest when she hadn't been able to hide.

And somehow, he seemed to bring that out in her. Because she wasn't able to hide her anger.

And she wasn't able to hide this. Whatever the wildness was that was coursing through her veins. No, she couldn't hide that either. And she wasn't sure she cared.

So she was just going to let the wildness carry her forward.

She couldn't remember the last time she had done that. The last time she'd allowed herself this pure kind of over-the-top emotion.

It had been pain. The pain she felt that night she lost the baby. That was the last time she had let it all go. In all the time since then when she had been on the verge of being overwhelmed by emotion she had crushed it completely. Hidden it beneath drugs. Hidden it beneath therapy speak.

She had carefully kept herself in hand since she'd gotten sober. Kept herself under control.

What she hadn't allowed herself to do was feel.

She was feeling now. And she wasn't going to stop it.

She launched herself forward, and her lips connected with his.

And before she knew it, she was kissing Jacob Dalton with all the passion she hadn't known existed inside of her.

Don't miss
Lone Wolf Cowboy *by Maisey Yates,*
available August 2019 wherever
Harlequin® *books and ebooks are sold.*

www.Harlequin.com

"To answer your other question," he murmured. "Why did I
single you out? Your first guess was correct. Because you are
so beautiful I couldn't help following you around this over-
the-top ballroom filled with people who possess more money
than sense. The women here can't outshine you. They're like
peacocks, spreading their plumage, desperate to be noticed,
and here you are among them, like the moon. Bright, alone,
above it all and eclipsing every one of them. What I don't
understand is how no one else noticed before me. Why every
man in this place isn't standing behind me in a line just for
the chance to be near you."

Silence swelled around them like a bubble, muting the din
of the gala. His words seemed to echo in the cocoon, and he
marveled at them. Hadn't he sworn he didn't do pretty words?
Yet it had been him talking about peacocks and moons.

What was she doing to him?

Even as the question echoed in his mind, her head tilted
back and she stared at him, her lovely eyes darker…hotter. In

that moment, he'd stand under a damn balcony and serenade her if she continued looking at him like that. He curled his fingers into his palm, reminding himself with the pain that he couldn't touch her. Still, the only sound that reached his ears was the quick, soft pants breaking on her pretty lips.

"I—I need to go," she whispered, already shifting back and away from him. "I—" She didn't finish the thought, but turned and waded into the crowd, distancing herself from him.

He didn't follow; she hadn't said no, but she hadn't said yes, either. And though he'd caught the desire in her gaze—his stomach still ached from the gut punch of it—she had to come to him.

Or ask him to come for her.

Rooted where she'd left him, he tracked her movements.

Saw the moment she cleared the mass of people and strode in the direction of the double doors where more tray-bearing staff emerged and exited.

Saw when she paused, palm pressed to one of the panels.

Saw when she glanced over her shoulder in his direction.

Even across the distance of the ballroom, the electric shock of that look whipped through him, sizzled in his veins. Moments later, she disappeared from view. Didn't matter; his feet were already moving in her direction.

That glance, that look. It'd sealed her fate.

Sealed it for both of them.

What will happen when these two find each other alone during the blackout?

Find out in
Black Tie Billionaire
by USA TODAY *bestselling author Naima Simone available September 2019 wherever Harlequin® Desire books and ebooks are sold.*

www.Harlequin.com